A MAN CALLED "WOZ"

He was a practical joker in high school, a college dropout, a compulsive daydreamer...and a millionaire many times over before he was thirty.

He walked away from his successful corporation, gave away large blocks of his Apple stock to friends and relatives, and spent millions on a rock festival.

He can easily afford to spend his life in leisure, but he's back at Apple, not as a corporate executive, but as a hands-on engineer, opening up manuals, conceptualizing, designing, deciding what chips to use. Steve Wozniak is back where he belongs.

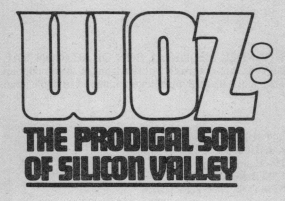

WOZ:
THE PRODIGAL SON
OF SILICON VALLEY

DOUG GARR

AVON
PUBLISHERS OF BARD, CAMELOT, DISCUS

WOZ: THE PRODIGAL SON OF SILICON VAL-
LEY is an original publication of Avon Books.
This work has never before appeared in book form.

AVON BOOKS
A division of
The Hearst Corporation
1790 Broadway
New York, New York 10019

Copyright © 1984 by Doug Garr
Published by arrangement with the author
Cover photograph by Mark Hanauer
Library of Congress Catalog Card Number: 84-91103
ISBN: 0-380-88484-4

          nting, September, 1984

For Meg

Acknowledgments

Several people made this possible, and I'd like to thank some of them: John McCollum, Randy Wigginton, Bill Fernandez, Chuck Mauro, and all the others at Apple, past and present, who took time out to be interviewed. Carol Mann, my agent, encouraged me to turn this into a book from a profile that originally appeared in *Omni* magazine. It was obviously a good idea. Of course, I'd like to thank Candi and Woz.

Contents

A mind forever voyaging through strange seas of thought...alone.

—from the original Apple Computer logo

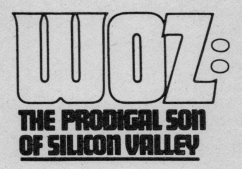

WOZ:

THE PRODIGAL SON OF SILICON VALLEY

Chapter One

Unity in the Dust Bowl

Devore, California, Labor Day weekend, 1982. The sun is high and the dust is kicking up as the wind blows off the San Bernardino hills. The temperature, mostly in the nineties and occasionally inching up to a hundred degrees, is parching the throats of some hundred thousand young people. The lemonade is two bucks a cup, but few people are complaining. Across the horizon sits a massive stage, 298 feet long, in an amphitheater—a shrine really, with a panoramic rainbow-colored swath of cloth. Off to one side, a Diamond Vision screen, the kind used in baseball parks, transmits the proceedings for the people in the back rows of sand, the cheap seats. Sting and the Police are powering through their dynamic repertoire on a 400,000-watt amplification system. The crowd, mostly wearing bathing suits or cutoff shorts and T-shirts, responds to the band's driving rhythms with a thunderous cheer across the fifty-eight-acre site. It is a monumental party in Southern California, and wafting in the distance is a multicolored hot-air balloon with the name "Apple Computer" below its midsection. The balloon is innocuous enough, at least amid the throngs, but it is also a not-too-subtle clue as to who paid for this shindig.

In the sixties there had been Woodstock, and in the seventies, Watkins Glen. Now, in the eighties, there was another rock-and-roll extravaganza, the US Festival, a three-day concert with an impressive array of acts: Fleetwood Mac, Talking Heads, Jackson Browne, Jerry Jeff Walker, Tom Petty and the Heartbreakers, Pat Benatar, the Charlie Daniels Band, and the B—52's, among them. The music itself had been arranged by Bill Graham, the aging rock impresario of the sixties and the man who brought us the Grateful Dead and other well-known rock bands from San Francisco. But music wasn't the only reason why these people were congregating. There was supposed to be something else for the cost of the tickets ($37.50 for the weekend, $17.50 for the day). The festival had been financed by a group called Unuson, an acronym for "Unite Us in Song." The whole idea was to usher a new concept into the decade. Americans love concepts and trends and labels, and what better way to attach meaning to a decade than with a rock concert? What better captive audience to hope for? After all, the sixties had peace and love and the seventies defined itself with selfishness (as the "me" decade, for want of a more benevolent identifier). The eighties must be accounted for early on; and they would have to connote something positive. The eighties, according to Unuson pamphlets, were to be the "Us" decade, an era when everyone wasn't so self-centered and uncaring, when people were righteous and friendly and cooperative. Help your fellow man instead of taking advantage of him. Somehow, the music would bring us together again.

The man primarily responsible for all this was Steve Wozniak, also affectionately known as "Woz," a compulsive daydreamer with a lot of free time. The rock extravaganza—cum-good-vibes might not have been a wholly original idea, but it certainly was a good start. Wozniak had spent the last year and a half recovering from an airplane accident and trying to decide what to do with the next portion of his life. In his first incarnation, he had been a computer engineer. He had invented a computer in his spare time and with a friend had started a company called Apple. Nearly a million people bought Wozniak's computer, making him a very wealthy man of leisure. One day, while cruising a freeway in Silicon Valley, he was listening to the radio, musing about his favorite rock bands. As a child of the sixties, albeit not a flower child, Wozniak longed for the era of the rock spectacular. Why not throw a concert, he thought? He knew nothing of the music business, but he could learn. He could teach himself, just as he had done designing computers. And if he had problems, he could hire the right people. Money was no obstacle.

Good enough, but not enough.

Wozniak had another idea as well. Why not introduce young America to technology? Throw a rock concert, but also put up tents where companies could show off their computer wares and other electronic consumer products. If the eighties were going to be meaningful, he reasoned, then microchips and rock and roll would have to learn to coexist. Togetherness. Among people and electronic circuitry and rock and roll. Woz wanted to create a "mini—World's Fair."

It was a grand scheme, and Wozniak needed a lot of help. He formed a corporation, Unuson, with a man named Peter Ellis and one of Ellis's friends, Gerald Cory. The company, however, was financed mostly with Wozniak's fortune. They found slick corporate offices in a modern building adjacent to the San Jose Airport. Peter Ellis was a smooth-talking ex-radical whose credentials were a Ph.D. and a track record of sixties activism. He had formed the San Jose chapter of Students for a Democratic Society, the most militant group of that era. Now he was an expert in extolling what many thought was a kind of new-age propaganda, love and peace eighties style. Ex-activists were now charming, sincere, positive-sounding, fitting into a mold cast by Tom Hayden. In reality, Ellis was little more than a representative of the pseudo-hip, laid-back life-style exemplified by the California ethos. Ellis was fond of "centering sessions," where you dissipated stress and tension "by holding hands and closing your eyes and hoping that things go well."

Right away there was tension. Wozniak wanted the best promoter to book his acts, so he hired Bill Graham. Graham, too, became famous in the sixties, but he was a straight-up businessman who once quit booking rock concerts because the musicians got too greedy. His attitude: You hire the band, secure a site, sell tickets, and give the crowd its money's worth. Peace and love was a nice idea, too, but it was a relic of past utopian dreamers. Graham didn't get along too well with Ellis. He had been to one of the Unuson centering sessions and was fairly disgusted with them. He decided not to close his eyes, peering instead at the others in the group. Graham thought that sitting and wishing away your problems was a ridiculous way to confront any crisis in a rock concert, whether it was something small (are there enough pay telephones for everyone?—apparently there weren't at first) or something big (I hope the Grateful Dead remember they have a gig this weekend).

In the middle of all this weird tension was Steve Wozniak. He had hired both Peter Ellis and Bill Graham. It was something like having your two grown children bickering with each other. Privately, his friends and family thought his throwing a rock concert was bizarre. After all, Steve's expertise was with a computer circuit board. Here he was investing some $12 million, and they thought it was nothing more than a fantasy, a party for his friends. Meanwhile, those close to him knew there was nothing they could do to persuade him not to do it. Because there were two absolutes about his personality that seemed to be unalterable. First, he was an extremely impressionable person. Wozniak was honest, open, trusting, and naive. Actually, all this to a fault. He liked to believe that everyone else was as right-thinking as he was. One former colleague, using the *Star Wars* trilogy as a metaphor, said, "The trouble with Wozniak is that he doesn't believe there's a Dark Side to The Force." People warned him that Peter Ellis might be the kind of person who would take advantage of his wealth, but Wozniak merely shrugged. Second, Wozniak was extremely compulsive when it came to getting something done. Once he decided he was going to do a project, he shifted gears into a quietly obsessive mode. Nothing was likely to change his mind or slow his pace until it was finished.

In order to throw a concert on the scale that Wozniak was thinking about, you needed to sell it. Before any acts were booked, Unuson hired a public relations consultant from Los Angeles, Bonnie Metzger. Metzger had considerable experience publicizing movies, but little in music. Still, after meeting Wozniak in his Berkeley apartment, she was impressed with his fresh, exuberant personality. "Woz was always himself," Metzger says. "That was what I was told he would be, and that rang true. He was exactly what he was at face value." There would be no need to craft an elaborate nice-guy persona, a media facade. Wozniak had no image, and he wasn't likely to acquire one. He agreed to do a month of interviews, and Metzger needed only to do "some grooming at first," and coach him a little for television interviews.

During the early part of 1982, the main problem in selling the US Festival was the fact that few people knew who Steve Wozniak was. Metzger found her press contacts more interested in his computer background than in his grandiose scheme to throw a rock concert. She had no choice but to take advantage of that. She suggested Wozniak put a "personal" message on computer disks and send them to the editors of the computer magazines. Woz was already well known in the relatively small computer community, and the editors were sure to be impressed by Wozniak's face on their monitors accompanied by a cute jingle promoting his newest venture. The first rumblings about Wozniak's new career surfaced in the trade press, and when Bill Graham began booking acts, the festival was on its way.

Wozniak decided to offer the first tickets to computer hobbyists by making an announcement on The Source, one of the nation's largest telecommunications networks. "We want to give them preferential treatment," he said.

19

Wozniak set out looking for a site. He flew his Beechcraft Bonanza from San Jose down to the Los Angeles Basin and located a prime spot to lease—the Glen Helen Regional Park—around sixty-five miles east of Los Angeles. Some 370,000 cubic yards of dirt would have to be moved to make room for the amphitheater, but that was no big problem. Woz made several other trips to Los Angeles city high schools, mostly to interview kids about what kinds of rock acts they liked best. It didn't take any measure of computer genius to discover that every teenager in the country wanted to see the "Boss." Wozniak offered Bruce Springsteen more than a million dollars, but Springsteen said no. Undaunted, Wozniak planned to pack them in anyway.

Wozniak was not naive in one respect. Since it was his first venture in rock promoting, he expected to lose money. He had to pay the bands alone $8 million for their services. If he broke even, he'd be happy. When asked by a *Los Angeles Herald Examiner* reporter what his motivation was, Woz was surprised at the question, as if one had to have a motive. He replied, "It's always a good time for a celebration. And I happen to have the resources to do it at this time. I'd like to attend something like this, and who is going to put it on if I don't?" In another interview Woz said, "We're simply planning on having a nice, peaceful day and smiling—the idea is to put smiles on everyone's face." He wanted to approach the spirit of Woodstock, so during his research he read *Barefoot by Babylon*, an account of that tumultuous, rainy weekend in 1969. "I never would have done this if I had read that book first," he would later comment.

When Labor Day weekend finally arrived, the relationship between the two organizing factions—Bill Graham and his Concerts West, and Unuson—had reached its nadir. Either Peter Ellis or Graham was going to be running the show, not both. Graham couldn't put up with Ellis's facade of trendy, soft-spoken togetherness, and Ellis couldn't understand why there was so much commotion. Graham threatened at one point to cancel all the bands. Wozniak's computer friends had trouble with their backstage credentials—indeed, the official passes changed daily—and there appeared to be a lot of confusion as to who was doing what. So much for the idea of togetherness and "us." At one point, Bill Graham fired Bonnie Metzger, who really became perplexed. She couldn't see how he could fire her; Unuson had hired her.

Woz, meanwhile, decided to ignore it as much as he could. He spent a lot of time perambulating the crowd, asking his patrons if they were enjoying themselves or if there were any problems. Wozniak's concerns were sincere, but his motive was also highlighted by yet another trait in his personality. When something gets to be a hassle, wipe it out of your mind. Avoid it, forget it, and hope it goes away, even if you know it won't.

Luckily, most of the divisiveness occurred behind the scenes, away from the crowd. Most of the concertgoers knew little about this ego-power struggle and probably wouldn't have cared. They were intent on ignoring the stifling heat and hearing some good music. Here, Woz didn't disappoint them. Nearly every critic was duly impressed by the clear and professional sound system, usually a problem at an outdoor concert. Few motorists had spent time stalled in traffic jams. Camping space was ample (recreational-vehicle capacity was estimated at a hundred thousand). There were enough beer and wine tents (four and a half acres' worth), water fountains, and portable johns to accommodate everyone. The joint technology-rock high point probably was reached when the Diamond Vision screen showed a Russian rock group, broadcast live from the Soviet Union. None of the American audience had ever seen what amounted to a communist version of the Rolling Stones.

The audience was perhaps bewildered by Wozniak's valiant attempt to integrate high technology with high-powered rock and roll. Though some appreciated the air-conditioned tents with their wondrous electronics displays, the great majority ignored them. They came to hang out. Who wanted to bother fussing around with computers at a rock concert? (Some musicians didn't seem to mind at all, however. Herbie Hancock and Chick Corea spent time lecturing on how they used computers to store sounds to help them compose.)

On September 3, in the middle of introducing the bands, Woz brought on stage the crowd's youngest patron, his son Jesse John Clark, born only hours earlier. At thirty-two, Woz was a father for the first time. He had insisted on giving Jesse his wife's surname, reasoning that it would be an unthinkable burden to walk around with a three-syllable name that no hotel clerk in the world seemed capable of spelling correctly. Yes, Clark was nice and simple and easy to spell. The diminutive, bearded Steve Wozniak, dressed in a casual T-shirt, tennis shorts, and his ever-present blue-and-white US baseball cap, gently cradled Jesse. Offstage, the proud mother, Candi, and the ebullient grandparents, Margaret and Jerry Wozniak, watched in wonder. How many kids are born at newsmaking rock concerts, they thought? There was a spirit of family about it.

After the show ended, Frank Sinatra's "My Way" blared over the speakers, an appropriate coda for the festival's organizers. Long after the helicopters had flown away the rock stars, long after the who's-in-charge-here bickering had waned to a reasonable level, and long after the last plastic garbage bag had been tied up, Wozniak's accountants began deciphering the numbers. Well, there would be huge losses, they decided, millions of dollars. Not enough people had turned out, they concluded. The crowd estimates had been hyped unrealistically. Some news accounts figured Wozniak lost around $10 million, and his family says the figure was higher, closer to $15 million.

It didn't make much difference to Steve Wozniak, however. He wanted to throw a party, get his own good seat (which he undoubtedly did), and make sure everyone had a good time. In fact, he even used the seat gambit in a subsequent TV commercial. Woz was shown onstage at the US Festival crowing about how he had to throw his own concert to get a good view of the proceedings. "I think the fans got their money's worth," he told reporters. "I know I got mine." He could afford this kind of glib comment because of a well-timed irony. During the period that Woz was blowing all sorts of money on the US Festival, Apple stock enjoyed a steady rally. It was estimated that his holdings increased in value by at least $18 million. When Woz said he was going to throw another concert the following year, there was no reason to doubt him.

Chapter Two

The Rites of Silicon Valley

Silicon Valley is hardly a valley in the traditional sense of geography. Physically, it covers the patch of land a half hour south of San Francisco, bordered by the city's bay and the low, rolling, foggy hills off the Pacific Ocean. Around three decades ago, what is basically Santa Clara County was burgeoning with peach and plum orchards, and the natives called it the Valley of Heart's Delight. Most of this rural character is gone, except for a few regions near the coastal plains. Arbitrarily, you can say that the valley covers about a hundred square miles. By the time you reach San Jose, you've already passed it. It got its nickname from a trade reporter in 1971, and the name stuck because it was a convenient way to refer to the high-technology industry that was growing there at a geometric rate. You can't build modern computers without integrated circuits or semiconductors, also known as "chips," with their wonderful, somewhat mysterious capacity for storing huge amounts of information. You need silicon to make chips, and silicon is extracted from sand, and there is an endless supply of that, and a seemingly endless demand to build chips.

Doug Garr

In the early days, Silicon Valley consisted of a few big electronics companies: Hewlett-Packard, IBM, Intel, National Semiconductor, Lockheed, Sanyo, Monsanto. Bill Hewlett and David Packard started in a garage back in 1939, and they are generally credited with beginning America's most daring computer migration. Life amid the eucalyptus groves at Stanford University has never been quite the same since. Before the defense industry went into its upswing-downswing cycles—meaning before the computer business was as sensitive to fluctuation in the economy as the rest of the nation's industries—there seemed to be a steady need for engineers. If you were a bright youngster getting a degree from Stanford or the University of California at Berkeley, you hit the freeways, either 101 on the east side or 280 on the west, and began dropping off resumes at some of the big outfits, or perhaps over at the National Aeronautics and Space Administration's Ames Research Center at the south end of San Francisco Bay. Aside from the linear accelerator in Palo Alto, Ames's huge hangar is probably the most imposing thing on the Silicon Valley horizon. Otherwise, the valley is a pretty routine version of suburbia, festooned with neatly landscaped lawns and ranch houses and palm trees. The bedroom communities have comfortable-sounding names like Sunnyvale, Santa Clara, Redwood City (where there are no redwood trees), Mountain View, Los Altos, and Cupertino.

Today, the valley is an array of electronic industrial offspring. New companies were born here during the silicon-chip rush. Mostly, they were started by restless engineers who wanted to become entrepreneurs. In order to attract venture capital, they took on serious, high-tech names, like "advanced" this or "superior" that, and inevitably had Z's or X's in their logos, like Zilog or Xedex.

The valley is going through middle-aged growing pains now. The electronic success stories—the ones that joke about how the Porsche is the official car of computer people and how the Jacuzzi is the official bathtub—are getting dated. The Silicon Valley millionaire

26

is merely a cliché, and the backlash—overwork, tension, a divorce rate that slips off the chart—is becoming a stern reminder that there is a price for everything involving the pursuit of the American dream.

By the time the personal-computer boom was upon us, Silicon Valley had taken on less of an elitist stance and gone more public. The semiconductor acquired a fascination for the layman, and, of course, the electronic marketeers took advantage of this. It is not startling to find a restaurant window displaying a menu done on computer printout. It certainly isn't intimidating to see a marquee sign along 101 that reads, "Double-density floppies, $29.95." We're supposed to know what that means. It's also not uncommon to hear a group of guys at lunch babbling stuff like, "God, did you see his code [computer program]? It's awful." Or, "I hear Osborne's having trouble going public." Or, "I never knew Woz wrote Little Breakout." A few years ago, you might have thought that the computer-controlled vending machines at Stanford's computer science building were a bit much, an unnecessary snub to the public at large. On second thought, though, it's rather more practical than clever, if you're a student. Punch in your password and order a bag of potato chips. You don't have to bother with a quarter because you'll get a statement on a printout every semester.

This was all a dream when Jerry Wozniak was an engineering student at the California Institute of Technology. In those days, computers were mammoth hunks of equipment, protected by large strips of sheet metal and cooled by noisy fans or Freon-filled air-conditioning pipes. They used vacuum tubes to help perform the arithmetic electronic chores, not silicon chips. In those days, even a transistor was a marvelous improvement and miraculous innovation in terms of miniaturization.

Jerry Wozniak is a calm and soft-spoken Californian with a preference for knit slacks and colorfully printed sport shirts with wide collars. He is employed by Lockheed, the huge aerospace firm, and when he's working on a sensitive government project he doesn't talk about it. When you're designing missiles, word gets around the neighborhood, and you don't just yak casually over dinner, not even to your wife. During the boom years of defense contracts, Jerry Wozniak sometimes put in sixty-hour weeks. The pace inevitably overwhelmed him. He had a heart attack. He's looking forward to retirement.

The Wozniaks' first child was born on August 11, 1950, at the San Jose Hospital. The announcement of the birth of Stephan Gary Wozniak was done on mock blueprint, featuring a caricature of a nineteen-inch-long baby "made by" Margaret and Jerry of "WOZNIAKS UNLTD." His mother was deeply interested in the arts, especially theater, and was hoping she would have an influence on his future choice of career. After all, his father would provide the science influence.

Steve Wozniak was a precocious youngster and a tinkerer extraordinaire almost as soon as he learned how to read. In fact, a lot of his early reading was in the engineering literature his father brought home from work. He became especially interested in ham radio, and built his own transmitter and receiver from a kit. He was only a sixth-grader when he earned his ham radio operator's license. A ham rating is not that easy to obtain. An applicant has to take a fairly difficult test in which he must demonstrate an overall knowledge of electronic theory and also send and receive telegraphically a minimum number of words per minute in international code. It's a lot like learning a second language. Wozniak mastered it when he was only eleven years old. When he got his license, Jerry Wozniak dutifully hoisted an antenna on the family roof. Richard Nixon, whose political career was far from finished, visited Sunnyvale. A picture of Steve with the future president ran in the local paper. Woz was offering Richard Nixon the support of the local ham radio operators. His mother recalls, "He built the radio, and then he lost interest in it. We knew he was intelligent, but you don't go around talking about it to your friends because, God forbid, everybody says that about their children."

Steve and, shortly thereafter, a brother Mark and sister Leslie grew up in a very middle-class neighborhood in Sunnyvale, the heart of Silicon Valley. Their brown wooden ranch home is on Edmonton Avenue, a quiet street with the usual quota of stray bicycles and station wagons. Steve spent much of his time lolling around his bedroom or on the living room rug, leafing through electronics magazines. He was developing his work habits without even knowing it. He spent long hours daydreaming or concentrating on a science project. Once started, it was difficult to pry him loose for dinner. His mother recalls having to hit him on the head to get his attention. The Wozniaks' eldest son had an uncanny ability to solve puzzles very quickly. He understood how things went together, and he frequently built kits correctly without even studying the diagrams. Right from the start, Woz understood spatial relationships. "When Steve got his Christmas toys, he'd start reading the instructions and he'd be lost," Margaret Wozniak says. "Instead of reading the instructions, he'd look at the toy and look at the parts, and whoosh, put it together, just like that."

"I had surfing posters in my bedroom when I was a kid," says younger brother Mark. "Steve had pictures of minicomputers from Data General." He was well on his way to becoming a certified electronics nerd, complete with a neatly shorn crew cut.

Still, Wozniak managed to enjoy a number of middle-American pursuits other than electronics. Jerry Wozniak was manager of the local Little League team, and Woz played a pretty fair shortstop. Steve hacked around the local tennis courts a bit, too. The Wozniak kids were animal nuts. Margaret remembers that Steve had an affinity for pet mice. He brought home a male (named Leonard), and his sister brought home a mate (Lolita, who turned out to be as sultry as her name), and the mice population just multiplied. There was even a white rat in the house, Hercules, who slept on his back with his feet in the air in the middle of Jerry and Margaret Wozniak's bed. Margaret Wozniak, who looks delicate and is less overweening about her children than her children think, said of her days as a zookeeper: "We always had animals around, everything but dogs because I was allergic to them. There was Myrtle the Turtle. I didn't think I could ever even touch a rat. But this one we had [Hercules] was one of the cleverest, smartest ones I'd ever seen. He even learned how to open his cage."

But it was electronics more than rodents that consumed Wozniak. In the early sixties, Steve was learning his way around transistors and capacitors and resistors, the miniature, color-coded parts that went into TV sets, radios, and other home appliances. Jerry Wozniak remembers teaching his son Ohm's law (a basic tenet of electrical theory), but beyond that Steve was mostly self-taught. When he wanted to know something, he consulted the appropriate manual. He rarely asked his dad for help. He built a primitive computer that played tic-tac-toe. His father still has it tucked away in the Wozniak garage.

By the time Woz got to the eighth grade, he was ready for his first serious computer project. For a science class at Cupertino Junior High School, he built a parallel digital computer, which, according to his father, didn't do very much but used advanced electronic circuitry. Jerry Wozniak recalls, "The significant thing about it was that integrated circuits were just starting to come out then [circa 1964], and he wrote a report that described a lot of stuff about computers; how diodes worked, how transistors worked, how gates worked. I had brought home a logic diagram from Texas Instruments and it showed how one of their modern, new integrated circuits worked—this was really new in those days—and they said this was the simplest possible circuit you can make. And he sat down with some transistors, diodes, and resistors we had obtained from local companies. And he designed one and it had fewer statements than that TI version. I said, 'You can't do it.' And he showed me how he made a gate with no transistors. And it worked. I went over the logic and it was absolutely solid. So it was a very simple, clean thing. He didn't just copy somebody else's idea."

His father, a seasoned engineer, was apparently impressed.

The people who judged the science fairs were also quite pleased. The parallel digital computer design won grand prizes at two local contests, and then took top honors at the Bay Area Science Fair. As a science-fair winner, Steve was treated to a day's tour of the U.S. Strategic Air Command facility at Travis Air Force Base. A ride in a noncommercial jet plane that day would have a lasting effect on him. He would catch the flying bug.

Jerry Wozniak still has a snapshot of his son demonstrating his invention. The thirteen-year-old Wozniak, neatly dressed in a white shirt with a cardigan sweater, is shown studiously pointing at his design.

A computer engineer was born.

Chapter Three

Funny Days
at Homestead High

Allen Baum, who is now an engineer with Hewlett-Packard, remembers meeting Steve Wozniak at Homestead High School, when they were juniors. "I went by his desk and saw him scribbling on a piece of paper, and I asked him what he was doing," he says. Without looking up, Wozniak replied, "Designing a computer." Oh, sure, Baum thought. Just like that. A computer. Baum, an electronics type himself, looked at the diagram. "It seemed like a copy of an existing computer, but it was still pretty impressive."

By now, Wozniak was pretty thoroughly familiar with the engineering basics of computing. He would spend the next few years honing his skills and developing his own ideas. He still played some tennis. Baum remembers that he favored a very aggressive game; he'd run anywhere for balls that seemed impossible to return. He was a master of the get, Woz himself says, but an overall mediocre player. What appealed to him was making a shot that appeared impossible to return. And he competed in the pole vault, though going to track practice was not a major priority. Mostly, Woz liked hanging out in Building F–3, Homestead's electronics laboratory.

F–3 was John McCollum's domain, and he presided there for over twenty years. McCollum, now sixty-two, finally retired last year because Homestead administrators tried to saddle him with too many students. The maximum his lab could handle was 130. They wanted him to teach 163. McCollum, with his thin graying hair, calculator wristwatch, and baggy trousers, reminds you of what television's Mr. Wizard probably would have looked like as he approached retirement age. An ex-navy pilot, McCollum always was accustomed to giving his students his complete attention. When the computer revolution moved into high gear, McCollum went back to school. He says he had to retrain himself four times to keep up with his students' demands. He had 164 sick days saved when he retired. "I could have taken off the entire last year," he says, referring to a chronic herniated disk condition. "But I wouldn't rip off the students." It isn't difficult to see why McCollum was Steve Wozniak's favorite teacher at Homestead. He represented inspiration and dedication.

Wozniak, of course, was also the kind of student who made an impression on McCollum. He took every electronics course the school offered for three years. When asked what kind of a pupil Woz was, McCollum didn't need to look up his grades. He remembers that he received all A's, and "could cool any test I could give him." There were other students in F–3 who were unusually bright. There was Greg Thompson, a young whiz who was sent to NASA's Ames Research Center to do independent computer work. Thompson went on to teach computer science at the Massachusetts Institute of Technology on the graduate level while only a freshman, McCollum recalls. Allen Baum, who would also go on to MIT, was also one of his top students. Though he won't admit to Woz being the best he's seen—there were some 2,500 students throughout his tenure—he does remember that the short, slightly stocky kid was unique. Woz was president of the Homestead Electronics Club and secretary-treasurer of the school's Math

Club. This second duty was a testament to his eclectic talent. Many kids who went through F–3 were destined to modest careers as electronics technicians. Important, yet humble. Technicians did some creative work in engineering labs, but mostly they were stuck doing chores that were considered too mundane for the top equipment designers. Lots of kids who took electronics courses didn't go to college. But if a student knew some math and electronics, he had engineer potential. Woz was the kind of math student who got an 800 on his college boards. And according to almost anyone who watched him work on one of F–3's long workbenches, he was one of the neatest and fastest guys with a soldering iron. So when Woz first arrived in McCollum's lab, there was absolutely nothing to intimidate him. None of the myriad electronic innards, like capacitors and resistors, could worry Woz, nor could the oscilloscopes, metering devices, and transmitters. He had already toyed with them while a junior high student.

McCollum insists that he spotted Wozniak's genius right away because of his penchant for pulling pranks. Most geniuses, he says, are very creative practical jokers. Thomas Edison, for one. Presper Eckert, the co-inventor of ENIAC, the first digital electronic computer, was another. "Woz told me he wanted to be remembered as the greatest practical joker that ever went to Homestead High," McCollum says. In a recent interview with his high school newspaper, it was the first thing Woz boasted about. "I claimed I was the greatest prankster ever in the school," he told *The Epitaph*. "I'm pretty sure the administration has records to this day that would classify me as one of the greatest."

He went about earning this honor with zeal. First Wozniak concentrated on the little annoyance gags, the kind that didn't require any electronics. He would write up three-by-five cards with a notice saying, "This class has been transferred to room L–20," and post them on classroom doors. Not only would the unsuspecting students obey the sign, but often the teacher did, too. Once, on the first day of school, Woz decided to redo the school's entire classroom schedule. The day before he had gotten hold of the master list, taken it home, and carefully recut and taped the room numbers and classes so they wouldn't correspond correctly. He then made about thirty-five photocopies of the altered list and returned to school at 2:00 A.M. He talked the janitor into letting him in, and surreptitiously posted all the new schedules. The chaos that ensued the next day was memorable, and Woz walked around as "confused" as all his schoolmates.

Wozniak has always taken pride in the fact that none of his pranks had any malicious intentions. One, however, was wrongly interpreted as having a less-than-honorable motive. He had built an electronic device that could trigger the fire alarm. He put a delay in it so, naturally, he could set the alarm off undetected. The day he chose to test it he was working after school in the electronics lab with four other students. It was a poor choice of location because McCollum was one of the few people smart enough to catch him. McCollum suspected the point of origin of the alarm was in F–3. "I knew it was false because nobody ran," he says. "Later, I got to thinking about it, and I called the principal and told him I had an idea who did it." The principal was furious, but McCollum said he wanted to take care of the disciplinary procedures by himself. The principal reluctantly agreed. McCollum then told Woz he wanted to "have a talk with him about the false alarm." Woz scurried away, displaying the cowardice of a guilty man. The teacher made no other mention of it. McCollum now laughs about the incident. "Whenever he gave me a hard time about anything, I threatened to tell on him," he says. "I held it over him for the rest of the school year."

Meanwhile, Woz occupied himself with lesser goofs. He built a frequency jammer, a devious little device that enabled him to disrupt the reception on a television set. Eventually, he got it down to such a small size that it could be disguised as an ordinary pen. He spent considerable time disrupting TV programs at friends' homes. When a show reached its crucial scene, oops—the picture disappeared. Or, he'd jam a picture and then wait for someone to tap the set or move the antenna. He'd turn off the jammer, and the picture miraculously reappeared. The electronic gremlins were stalking the TV tubes, all at the behest of Woz. When he was really adept at it, he could get someone to assume silly, contortionist-like positions while trying to keep the TV from going wild. McCollum knew about the jammer, but kept it quiet, even when Woz worked his magic on one of the English teacher's TV sets. "I figured if I go rat on him," McCollum says, "I'd never find out about some of these things." McCollum was beginning to preside over a cadre of court jesters, led by Wozniak. One Woz confederate figured out how to move all the school's clocks ahead an hour (to get home from school early, one presumes), but McCollum had to put a stop to it because that kind of disruption was really frowned on by the principal.

Steve Wozniak was certainly alleviating the school's ennui, as well as his own. McCollum describes his talent as being prodigious but also untapped and undisciplined. Woz had a lot of energy and ambition—he wanted to be either an engineer or a teacher—but he had a certain streak of laziness. He was a classic example, in the parlance of educators, of not "working to his potential." The reason was, of course, that his potential was so awesome. Still, McCollum was flattered that his class was the only one Woz wouldn't cut. But his antics and cavalier attitude to formal schooling also worried McCollum. The teacher vividly remembers the following conversation with his star pupil.

McCOLLUM: Woz, you're not going to graduate from college.
WOZNIAK: Why?
McCOLLUM: Because you won't put up with all the folderol the professors are going to throw at you.
WOZNIAK: I can graduate from any college I want.
McCOLLUM: Sure, but you won't.

"He couldn't comprehend what I was driving at," McCollum says.

When it came to legitimate extracurricular activities, Woz was an inspiration and a natural leader. As head of the Electronics Club he set up field trips on several occasions. Because of Woz, the club got to tour Fairchild's Research and Development Center, where the members saw state-of-the-art work in electronics.

Woz was well liked by his peers, but they also held him in some kind of awe, which surprised McCollum. "I've had other kids equally brilliant," he says. "But in a different direction."

Largely because of his father and his interest in electronics field trips, Woz became the consummate forager for parts. Jerry Wozniak knew Gordon Moore, who had co-founded Fairchild and was now chairman of Intel. Jerry had worked with Moore on guidance systems, and when his son wanted to fool around building gizmos, he would call Moore and scrounge for reject diodes and resistors and the like. He brought them to school and started a new project. He was always working on some kind of electronic box. "This was his fun class," McCollum said. "He had free rein here. He went off farther than our facilities could provide." When Woz reached his senior year, there was pretty much nothing more McCollum could teach him about computers. So he arranged to send Woz to Sylvania, where he spent an hour a week on a large main-frame system. Woz was now on an independent study program. When he was finished, McCollum asked him to prepare a lecture. Woz taught class one day, and he was good.

The prima donna in him remained active. During one lecture, McCollum went into a long dissertation on some aspect of electrical theory. Woz walked into class a few days later holding a manual with an ancient copyright date which disproved everything McCollum said. And when the teacher asked his class for a three-page paper explaining how integrated circuits worked, Wozniak was so enthusiastic he turned in thirty-five pages. It was clearly, simply written. His grade was an A+.

The pranks, naturally, also went on. Wozniak's tour de force was also the only one he actually got caught at. One of his friends had seen a circuit diagram in an electronics magazine that showed how to build a high-frequency oscillator. When you turned it on, it was supposed to sound like a leaky faucet, "drip-drip-drip." Woz decided to build it. When it was finished, it sounded more like a loud clock that went "tick-tick-tick." In fact, if you put some tinfoil around it and hooked up some wires, you might be able to make someone think it was a bomb. The devious side of Woz took hold of him, and he did just that. He knew the combination of one of his friends' lockers, so he opened it and placed his bogus explosive in it. The area high schools were getting a lot of bomb scares in those days, and it was no trouble at all to create one at Homestead. When the principal had the locker opened and discovered the ticking device, he quickly took it out to the football field where he courageously "dismantled" it. It didn't take long to discover he had been duped by one of his students. Because of Wozniak's reputation, the principal knew immediately where to round up the usual suspects. In this case, however, there was only one. Woz was hauled into his office. Since other's were involved in the ruse, Woz suspected someone had snitched. Enraged, the principal elicited a confession. Woz was sent to the Juvenile Hall section of the local police department. When Margaret Wozniak heard her son had been arrested, she too was furious. Her son a criminal? She bailed him out and the misunderstanding was finally cleared up. When Woz returned to school, the news was all over the place. For his deed, he received a standing ovation in one class.

Wozniak's guidance counselor suggested, quite seriously, that he undergo psychiatric care.

Today, F–3 has a kind of underground status in Silicon Valley. McCollum is proud that five of Apple Computer's first eight employees went through there. There is even an homage to the computer boom in the lab. Next to the teacher's desk stands an ancient video game, Flim-Flam, donated by one of McCollum's former students who now works for Atari. Basically, it was the forerunner of Pong, the first successful arcade game. It costs the kids only five cents a play. It is truly an electronic museum piece.

Chapter Four

The Cream Soda Computer

Steve Wozniak graduated from Homestead High in June 1968 with a pretty good academic record. A tad short of excellent, actually. He had received four small scholarship awards in math and electronics, and a grant from the National Science Foundation stemming from an advanced math class at the University of Santa Clara. He was listed in *Who's Who in American High Schools*. He was a member of the National Honor Society and the California Scholarship Federation. His B's in humanities courses combined with A's in math and electronics brought him a class rank in the top 10 percent. He was prouder, naturally, of his unofficial merry-prankster record. And though the fifty-dollar cash award he won from the Mount Diablo Computer Programming Contest along with a twenty-five-dollar savings bond from the National High School Math Contest were small compensation for his long labors, he was pleased with his success. Clearly, he was headed for greater awards. Money wasn't a problem or a priority, anyway. His family was hopelessly middle class.

Woz tended to migrate toward friends with similar

hobby interests, so he formed a natural partnership when he met a neighbor, Bill Fernandez, who was a few years younger. Fernandez lived in a house across the way from the Wozniaks in a quiet little cul-de-sac. His father was a locally prominent lawyer and is now a superior-court judge in Santa Clara County. He knew Woz's dad had gone to Cal Tech and worked for Lockheed. Bill was low-key and shy, but he had an avid interest in electronics which really began to mature when he was a high school freshman. Woz showed Fernandez his projects, including his first computer with "primitive" diodes and transistors and his tic-tac-toe computer. Fernandez was eager to learn more, and Woz gladly shared his vast knowledge. Woz showed him how to warble the sound on a siren, for example.

The main thing that Woz taught Fernandez, however, was how to infiltrate the system to get electronic parts for free. You have to remember that these kids had no steady income other than their allowances, and parts were expensive. Some were difficult to get anyway. Fernandez and Woz were far more advanced than the conventional hobbyists who spent their Saturdays browsing the racks at Radio Shack and Lafayette Electronics. Fernandez was surprised that Woz had such a smooth-flowing pipeline to the various Silicon Valley companies. Monsanto, Fairchild, Signetics, Intel—it didn't really matter. Woz would check out an intriguing circuit diagram and then a catalogue and pick up the phone. His pitch invariably contained the following: he was an underprivileged high school student interested in electronics; he had to have this relay or that diode; and he was desperate. Was there anything lying around a bin that hadn't passed inspection that still worked? Any surplus or discontinued parts? So while Fernandez was impressed with Wozniak's collection of contraptions, he had a greater admiration for his charm and ability to immediately assemble an inventory of parts. Woz was a computer nerd, but he wasn't an ordinary one.

"He called up Fairchild and got thousands of transistors," Fernandez says. "One day, he called Signetics and asked them for all their surplus parts. Then he called Intel and Monsanto and did the same thing. When they arrived, he took them over to my house and dumped them on the living room floor. He took out the catalogue and labeled all the counters, multiplexers, latches, shift registers. Then he said, 'Hey, we have everything we need to build a computer.' A day later, he came back with a schematic diagram to do it."

To say that Wozniak had nerve is probably an understatement. He was going to build a computer totally from parts cadged from Silicon Valley dumping bins. To be fair, Fernandez and Wozniak probably should have called their proposed invention the Monsanto-Fairchild-Signetics-Intel computer, but that would've sounded a bit cumbersome, not to mention brash. Fernandez had a better idea for a name. They spent almost all their summer weekends spread out on Fernandez's garage workbench, and their subsistence beverage was Cragmont cream soda. (Computer devotees seem to zealously favor junk food and soda pop, as we shall soon illustrate.) They dubbed their invention the "cream soda" computer. Not very commercial, but it made their point. The machine was simple and small, remembers Fernandez. The mother board (also known as a "bread board")—the central processing unit—was designed by Woz because he had a greater knowledge of digital electronics. It had eight integrated circuits and measured four and a half by seven inches. Fernandez built the power supply. He remembers that Woz had unusual skill in using parts for tasks other than their intended design. His digital design ability was astounding. Of course, this computer was nothing like a business machine. It didn't do much but add, subtract, multiply, and divide numbers. But it had light-emitting diodes—those tiny red bulbs you find on some wristwatches to display the time—so it was something to look at.

Woz's mother, the duo's greatest supporter, decided to call up the *San Jose Mercury* to get some publicity. She invited a photographer to the house to document their invention. When he arrived, the two gingerly turned on the machine. To their monumental disappointment, it didn't work. Fernandez remembers it as such a spectacular failure for one reason. Usually, when a computer breaks down or doesn't start, absolutely nothing happens. No big bursts of energy or rumblings or shakings, as Hollywood movie producers would like us to believe. The cream soda computer, however, was different. It started smoking. One of the integrated circuits—it was now obvious why it had been in a company's throw-away bin—wasn't working. They tried and tried, probably to the point where the power supply overheated. But it was no go. The *Mercury* photographer left without clicking his camera shutter.

Steve Wozniak shrugged off the bum computer. After all, he knew why it hadn't worked. His electronic theory was sound, and that was of far greater importance.

Meanwhile, Bill Fernandez didn't know it, but he was about to have a profound influence on the computer industry. Some time later, he was to meet another Homestead High student named Steven Jobs. Fernandez and Jobs had two things in common: first, they were both interested in electronics, and second, they both had an affinity for Eastern philosophy. Fernandez, tall and thin with black hair, is the kind of person who, you immediately discover, has an exact perspective on his own life. He is in control. He's a faithful vegetarian. After earning an engineering degree he was hired by Hewlett-Packard, where he worked in the Advanced Products Division. He spent two years living in Japan, and is fluent in Japanese, having studied the language and the country's culture prior to his trip.

Steven Jobs had a healthy teen-aged affection for Zen, but it resulted more from his being a hippie in the middle-class sense of the word, circa 1970 in California. Jobs wore his hair long and favored patched jeans and sandals. He wasn't in the habit of taking showers, and acquaintances do not hesitate to say he smelled like it. The best time to bump into Jobs was after he came out of swimming practice.

Steve Wozniak went to the University of Colorado and signed up for a joint major in electrical engineering and computer science. He didn't exactly spend a lot of time in class, however. When he wasn't learning how to ski, he took his TV jammer into the dorm lounge and put his fellow freshmen through the contortionist antics that he had choreographed so well. He started sending ham radio signals through the dorm, disrupting everyone's radio and TV reception. This went on for quite some time. When the dorm formed a vigilante committee to catch the intruder, Woz, to his profound delight, was named a member. He brought home a couple of gerbils on vacation (illegally; California doesn't allow rodents to cross its border) and told his family he wouldn't return for his sophomore year. The Wozniaks were prepared for the announcement. They knew their son had difficulty applying himself. Jerry Wozniak says that if Steve was interested in a course, he got an A. If he was bored, he was easily capable of flunking it. He also missed the familiar surroundings of Silicon Valley. He decided to attend De Anza, a local college.

It was at about this time that Bill Fernandez introduced Wozniak and Jobs to each other. Jobs had been at Bill's house, so he decided to call Woz and invite him over. "They had two things in common," Fernandez says. "They were both into electronics, and they both liked to pull pranks." The two had distinctly different personalities—Woz was quiet and Jobs was extremely extroverted. Woz was sort of a loner and Jobs was gregarious. Jobs loved to be the center of attention and insisted on getting his own way. Wozniak didn't care. His ego was subdued. In the jargon of the day, Woz was "mellow" and Jobs was "hyper." At first, it seemed like an unlikely friendship. Sure, they liked mischief and gadgets, but Woz was well steeped in electronic theory, and Jobs's interest was merely casual. Jobs was more likely to be found playing with a gadget than building it. Eventually, their disparate skills and personalities would complement each other. At the time, they didn't know their alliance would some day burgeon into one of the greatest success stories in the computer industry and American business.

Bill Fernandez wouldn't be forgotten either. He eventually earned the distinction of becoming Apple Computer's first employee.

Chapter Five

The Blue-Box Capers

Steve Wozniak spent the following year at De Anza College, but then abruptly decided to transfer to Berkeley. He was committed to engineering, and he couldn't apply himself at a tiny place like De Anza. Berkeley wasn't nearly as prestigious as Stanford, but it had one of the better computer science–electrical engineering programs.

The sixties weren't yet a decade—that is, we didn't call them "the sixties." But by 1971, the nation's college students had gone through much of their political-awareness pain and suffering. The People's Park fiasco in Berkeley (resulting in a protester's death) was recent history. So too was the Kent State disaster, indirectly caused by Vietnam war protests, which left four dead. None of this mattered much to Woz. He ignored the newspaper headlines. The voting age had been lowered from twenty-one to eighteen by a stroke of Richard Nixon's pen, but Woz hardly noticed. He couldn't have cared less about politics, and he was too cynical to bother voting. He was the kind of student who walked around with a slide rule on his belt.

Woz was more intrigued about what was happening

in the world of electronics. Engineers were making great strides in integrated circuits. The circuits were getting physically tinier, moving larger amounts of information in and out of computers faster, and perhaps most important, they were becoming cheaper because of greater demand. The potential for miniaturization in electronics fascinated Woz. Consumer electronics pundits were predicting future low prices on a chip known as LSI (for "large-scale integration") and an even more sophisticated one called VLSI (for "very large-scale integration"). Applications were limited only by a company's imagination. Every kind of consumer product involving electronics would be affected. They would get smaller and cheaper, and most importantly, they would be more reliable because they would contain fewer parts. Everything would be touched by new technology; stereo gear, portable radios, and TV sets. Calculators, which had replaced the slide rule as the main number-manipulating tool of science students and engineers, and electronic watches were still very expensive, costing hundreds of dollars. Soon, middle-class folks like Steve Wozniak would be able to afford them. Also, Woz knew, someday he wouldn't have to scrounge for parts to build computers—or any other electronic gadgets.

One day in October 1971, Margaret Wozniak was leafing through *Esquire* magazine. Since she was the family member who was most interested in politics and culture, she kept up with the latest periodicals. She noticed a story called "Secrets of the Little Blue Box." The piece didn't interest her very much, but she thought her son might like to read it. She sent Steve a copy. Woz read through a very detailed account of an outlaw band of pranksters who defrauded the telephone company by making illegal long-distance phone calls with the aid of an electronic box. They weren't part of a conspiracy per se, but they talked with each other nationwide on a regular basis to exchange technical information about the phone company's vast computer network. They called themselves "phone freaks." They were to become the new-age hippies. It wasn't drugs that turned them on; it was the clicks and tones of Ma Bell's computers.

According to the *Esquire* article, the phone company

had made a multi-billion-dollar commitment to operate its switching system on a series of tones. One part of the system, which connected the company's complex trunk lines through switching offices, was based on a 2600-cycle frequency. The offices had lines called tandems, which managed incoming and outgoing long-distance calls. When one trunk was busy, the computer automatically switched a call to the next most convenient one that had an open line. Thus, if you were calling Los Angeles from New York and a trunk line in Kansas City was overcrowded with long-distance calls, your call might be automatically switched through Minneapolis or Dallas depending on the traffic density. All this information, unfortunately for the phone company, was a matter of public record. It had been previously published in a technical journal and was available to anyone who cared enough to make a trip to the library. And it was too late to change it.

It was all very involved technically, but these electronic wizards figured out how to use the 2600-cycle tone to receive free phone calls. A freak known as Captain Crunch (all the people in the story had pseudonyms) had discovered that the whistle in a Cap'n Crunch cereal box tooted an exact 2600-cycle tone. When his friends called him, he beeped the whistle into the receiver and somehow the incoming caller's billing code disappeared. Captain Crunch could receive free calls from anywhere in the world. It wasn't long until Captain Crunch and his cohorts figured out how to build an electronic device to manipulate the phone company signals to gain access to various 800 (toll-free) numbers. Captain Crunch was the expert at this sort of thing, and he was apparently so addicted to phone freaking that he amused himself by calling the U.S. Embassy in Moscow via satellite just to chat about the weather. Or, he'd stand in a telephone booth and call the booth next to him by latching into tandems all over the world. If his connection circled the earth enough times, there was a twenty-second or so transmission delay. The delay actually allowed him to talk to himself!

Woz finished the article and, fascinated with the electronics, decided he had to meet Captain Crunch. But how? He wasn't exactly listed in the telephone directory. The article had revealed Crunch as an engineer with a strange personality. The phone company had been battling back with its own detection devices and was on to the freaks' schemes. They were close to catching Crunch and the others. Invariably, when an outsider wanted to talk or meet with the Captain, he became wary and unequivocally stated that he wasn't involved any more. Then, when his paranoia began to wane, he dropped his guard and would start bragging about his latest pranking exploits, babbling like crazy.

Meanwhile, Wozniak found the blue-box technology intriguing enough to try and build one himself. He took a trip to the library, browsed through the phone company manuals, and went to work. Steve Jobs had begun hanging around Wozniak's Berkeley dorm room, and he, too, was interested. When Woz finished his invention, he didn't know how to use it. The *Esquire* piece had furnished almost all the frequencies, the critical blue-box operating information, but Woz needed certain codes to dial other countries. Right now, it was a limited tool. For the box to be really useful, you had to be able to use the system transglobally. He needed Captain Crunch, or someone with his knowledge, to show him how the box worked.

As publicity about phone freaks grew, Wozniak and Jobs kept up with all the latest stories. The two had been trying to meet Captain Crunch for the longest time. One day, Jobs learned that Crunch had done an interview on a Los Gatos radio station. They tried to track him through the station but failed. Finally, they got a lead through a miraculous stroke of luck. Wozniak recalls, "A friend of mine from high school dropped by my dorm and said, 'I know who this guy Captain Crunch is. His name is John Draper. He works for KKUP radio in Cupertino.' So we called KKUP that night, and they said he dropped out of sight right after the *Esquire* article, or something." Wozniak left his dorm phone number, and eventually John Draper called him. Woz excitedly told him that he had read all the stories, that he had built his own blue box, and that he wanted to meet with him. Draper went into the same spiel that was in the *Esquire* story. I'm not interested in messing around with the phone company, he said. I think Ma

Bell is very good for the country. I don't do any phone freaking any more. I don't do blue boxes. Besides, he warned Wozniak, it's much too dangerous and easy to get caught. But eventually Crunch relented and made a date to visit Wozniak and Jobs at Berkeley. Later, Woz realized that Crunch behaved strangely partly because he thought the phone company and other authorities were using fronts, innocent people, to infiltrate his activities. Once Draper was fairly certain it wasn't the cops on the phone, he'd revert to his usual crazy persona.

When Draper, who was then thirty-one, met the two aspiring phone freaks, he went through his entire repertoire. They retreated to a phone booth, and the Captain called all over the planet, stacked up tandems, and demonstrated his latest no-cost dialing techniques. "That one night he gave us everything," Wozniak says. Draper's machine was pretty sophisticated, remembers Woz, but it was bulky and quite expensive. The parts cost Crunch around $1,500. Wozniak showed Draper his blue box, which was smaller and contained only $40 in electronics. Woz was pleased. When Draper left, Jobs and Wozniak tested their machine, and it worked very well. Today, Wozniak reminisces about the box with relish. "Every phone freak in the world who's ever built a box thinks mine is the best design in the world," he says. "I think it's one of the best electronic designs I've ever done in my life, to tell you the truth."

Jobs and Wozniak decided to start their first business venture together, building and selling blue boxes. The boxes, of course, were highly illegal. (Woz disputes this, saying it wasn't necessarily a crime to build or own one. It was stealing phone calls that was illegal.) The economics were uncomplicated. They sold them "wholesale" for about $80, and the subsequent seller got about $150. Their net profit was only about $20 apiece per box, but they were happy. Woz and Jobs sold the boxes by word of mouth or door-to-door at Berkeley dormitories. Wozniak was so confident of his product that he guaranteed the blue box for life just like a Zippo cigarette lighter. "I offered a total warranty, a total repair," he said. If it broke, the "distributor" could return it to him and he would fix it free. Inside each box,

Woz inserted a card that read, "He's got the whole world in his hands." It was a joke on the phone company, of course, but it also identified each Wozniak-Jobs box.

Draper remembers that when he first met Jobs and Wozniak they were an inseparable pair. "They were Mutt and Jeff," he says. "I wouldn't see one without the other." Once he did hang out with Wozniak alone, when the two went to the Stanford engineering library to check out some technical information. "He'd understand all the formulas," Draper marvels about Woz. "I wouldn't understand too much of what was going on." Draper was totally against selling the boxes, and he told Woz so. But Wozniak ignored him.

Word of the two Steves' business quickly filtered south to Silicon Valley, and more than a couple of pairs of eyebrows were raised. When they visited Homestead High, John McCollum was quite concerned. He had had Jobs as a student, too, and though Jobs didn't have the technical brain that Woz did, McCollum does remember him as competent enough to get B's. McCollum remembers that Jobs had trouble taking criticism. "He'd go into a snit if I said anything bad about his work," he says.

McCollum sternly lectured Wozniak and Jobs; building blue boxes was hardly the thing they should be involved in. The teacher warned Woz that if he wasn't careful, Ma Bell was going to catch him. Woz countered by saying he wasn't really doing anything that bad. He was building and selling an electronic device. He wasn't encouraging anyone to break the law. Besides, he did not use his own blue box to make free calls to his friends. He was scrupulously insistent on paying his own phone bill, which was running about a hundred dollars a month. He did use the box, however, to "explore the system," to learn more about Ma Bell's far-reaching computer tentacles.

Wozniak and Jobs ignored McCollum's advice, naturally, and by doing so they almost ran into trouble. The two almost did get caught, right at the beginning of their venture. One night they were driving on a freeway in Hayward when their car broke down. They limped into a rest area and decided to use the blue box to call for help. A highway patrol car pulled up to make a routine check. They were about to panic when Jobs gave the box to Woz to hide, and he put it in his pocket. One officer searched him and found it.

"What's this thing?" the policeman asked.

"It's just a synthesizer," Woz quickly replied. "It makes music." He then pressed all the tone buttons used to dial calls. They thought everything was all right until the other cop asked what the orange button was used for—the one that actually tapped into the phone system for free calls. Jobs jumped into the conversation and gave them a line about "calibrating" the tones. The two were praying that they wouldn't be arrested. How much did the average cop know about blue boxes, they were thinking, while their pulses raced? The patrolmen seemed skeptical, but they finally returned the box to them.

One officer said, "A guy named Moog already beat you to it."

In a moment of relief and unable to resist a comment, Jobs said, "Oh, yeah, we sent him our schematic diagram."

Meanwhile, Wozniak had become pretty friendly with John Draper. The two could talk for hours about highly technical phone company doings, or computers, or anything electronic. Woz brought Captain Crunch to his Edmonton Avenue home. Eventually, Draper met Woz's folks. Margaret Wozniak was not immediately (or ever) charmed by the Captain. He was seven years older than her son and seemed a little flaky. Her friends thought Steve was a little eccentric, she thought, somewhat aghast. What would they say if they met Captain Crunch?

When she found out about the blue-box business Woz was involved in, she was not happy at all. Draper was a bad influence on her son. No doubt she was reminded of the "bomb scare" Wozniak had pulled in high school and the trouble it nearly caused. When Draper asked to use the Wozniak telephone, she balked. After all, this wasn't just *anybody* asking to borrow your phone. This was the Billy the Kid of the trunk lines. "Every time the phone rang in the middle of the night, I thought it was the police," she says. "I forbade him [Steve] from using my telephone for illegal purposes."

Woz's younger brother Mark was a high school student, and though he wasn't much of an electronics buff, on occasion he enthusiastically hit the blue-box buttons. He was on the school swim team with Steve Jobs, so he kept up with his brother's activities even while Woz was in Berkeley. When the Sunnyvale phone freaks gathered—Draper, Jobs, Woz, and Mark—they thought of all kinds of pranks they could pull with the boxes. What if they could "busy out" an entire city? Why they could start with a relatively modest-sized one, like San Jose, and tie up all its trunk lines. Wouldn't it be a gas if nobody could dial into San Jose because every phone was "busy"? They never did manage that feat, but it illustrates just how imaginative they were.

Woz actually did try to pull another particularly noteworthy trick. He called the Vatican in Rome and asked to speak to Pope Paul VI. When one of the papal assistants asked who was speaking, Woz said he was Secretary of State Henry Kissinger, using his best voice imitation. It didn't work. The assistant knew what the real Kissinger sounded like, and he was disconnected.

Back at Berkeley, the blue-box business boomed. Woz and Jobs went from building them singly to assembling them ten and twenty at a time. Jobs was the guy who wanted to accelerate production. "He was the one pursuing it," said Wozniak. "He was always saying, 'Will you take ten, will you buy twenty?' He was very business-minded." He was so aggressive, Wozniak thought, that if it hadn't been so chancy, he'd probably have wanted to incorporate and advertise. Still, Wozniak's contacts meant more in sales. He met a phone freak in Los Angeles one night on a "loop-around" call who led him to another contact. Jobs apparently got nervous about the business, and his girl friend objected to his involvement. She tried to get him to bow out. "He was happy to take half the money," Woz said. So he stayed in. The two eventually sold around two hundred before they closed up shop.

Some people did get caught defrauding the phone company with Wozniak's blue box. Gail Fisher, the actress who played Mannix's secretary in the TV series, and Bernard Cornfield, the get-rich-quick financier, were among a number of celebrities who were nailed by authorities. Wozniak did not sell them boxes directly. "One of the guys I was selling blue boxes to told me about these celebrity circles he was running in," Woz said. He never thought much about all the name-dropping, and he never really knew whether the guy was selling to them. "Oddly enough, when I started reading the newspapers, all the ones he had mentioned were getting busted. In a couple of cases, I heard through the right channels that it was my box."

When *Omni* magazine published a story about Wozniak in 1983, it mentioned his blue-box exploits. Shortly thereafter, he began receiving phone calls from young people who wanted the frequencies and codes of the phone company. He answered as many inquiries as possible and encouraged them as long as they were juveniles and not adults. Woz said, "I asked their ages. I figure if they're young enough, let 'em go. Because even if they get caught, what happens to them? You know, you get caught, you're probably never going to do it again. They'll talk to you, slap your wrist, and say, 'Don't do it any more.' And they'll probably never do it any more. Even Crunch was thirty-seven years old. Three times he had to get busted before he went to prison." Wozniak also approves of kids who pirate computer programs. It's not so much that he's altruistic about it—they can't afford them, so we should overlook it if they steal—but because he feels society will eventually benefit. Some day, they may do something useful and knowledgeable because of it. The good in it all will come to pass if we're patient.

The end of the blue-box era, for Wozniak and Jobs, came in 1973. They had outgrown the pranks and knew all the intimate and worthwhile secrets that had emanated from Bell Laboratories. Even John Draper realized there was no real future in phone freaking. How much time could Captain Crunch spend talking to himself on forty tandems, anyway? Draper and Wozniak would stay in touch. It certainly was to Draper's advantage. According to Mark Wozniak, "Draper was in outer space, in another galaxy. My brother was the only guy who could keep him from cracking up."

This period, the early seventies, took on an important meaning. Technology was no longer an ominous, foreboding shadow hidden behind the government and corporate facade. It didn't necessarily represent Big Brother. The Vietnam war was winding to a close. So what if Saigon was to be renamed Ho Chi Minh City? The Cambodian atrocities were still to come, but people were beginning to grow weary of protesting. Watergate would entertain us for only two years. There was no real cause any more, no flagpole to rally around. It was time to take stock of your life. It was considered a propitious idea to self-actualize—the seventies catch phrase that translated into growing up, finding a career, and earning a fulfilling living. It was a new era for the nation's youth. It was still all right to listen to rock and roll. But technology was going to be the new addiction. Marijuana wasn't going to slip out of vogue, but the microchip, containing those tiny integrated circuits that could do so many things, would certainly be an adequate replacement. The "hacker" would eventually supplant the hippie. It was time to seize some of this circuitry.

Chapter Six

Brews, Victuals, and Home Computer Stews

John McCollum's sermonette to Steve Wozniak about his not graduating from college was beginning to look like an astute prophecy. Woz had spent so much time with the blue boxes that he was having trouble maintaining interest in school. Besides, he was already working. One summer he got a job at American Micro Systems, and even though he wasn't a bona fide engineer, he often did the work of one. During another summer, Woz worked at an electronics firm in Palo Alto. He was gaining valuable experience designing and laying out printed circuit boards. Though he was called a technician, he impressed his superiors and was given greater responsibilities. He was promised a promotion to engineer, but the company went out of business before the change came through.

What Woz really wanted to do was work for Hewlett-Packard. H-P was the prestige company in Silicon Valley, and Woz knew he was good enough to work for the best. What he wasn't so willing to do was stay in college long enough to get his electrical engineering degree. He interviewed at H-P in three different divisions. The company liked him, knew instantly that he was an extraordinary talent, and hired him even though he had no degree. He was 23 years old. His high school buddy Allen Baum was working in the company's Research and Development Division, where all the brainstorming went on. Woz apparently wasn't qualified for that department, but Baum helped him get a position in the Advanced Products Division. Though he wasn't a fully vested engineer, he worked as one, solving design problems on new calculators. Since Woz was also a consummate math buff, he was extremely happy with the job.

Meanwhile, video games were beginning to take off. A young Silicon Valley engineer named Nolan Bushnell had begun marketing Pong, an electronic Ping-Pong game. Developed in 1972, the game began appearing in pubs in 1973, and a year later the same technology evolved into other games. The future would see all kinds of space-wars games with colorful graphics. The pinball machine was beginning to look like a relic. The "ka-ching" sounds of steel balls hitting rubber bumpers were giving way to strange-sounding beeps, at a pitch that was soon identifiable as computer-generated. Bushnell called his firm Atari, and eventually sold it to Warner Communications for $26 million. In five years, the video arcade would have a massive economic impact in the entertainment business. In its peak year, coin-operated video games would outgross the nation's movie business. The spectacle of the under-forty (soon to be under-thirty) Silicon Valley millionaire was becoming commonplace. Nolan Bushnell, after all, was only twenty-eight when he began fantasizing about the video-game business.

Steve Jobs didn't fit very well into the collegiate mold. He didn't like formal academia any more than Woz. He spent two years at Reed College in Oregon and dropped out. Eventually, he followed his Zen instinct to a logical conclusion. He journeyed to India in search of a guru and the meaning of life. Jobs, however, was too tightly wound up mentally and emotionally to waste time meditating for six hours a day. Undoubtedly, part of his great awakening pointed to the grim reality that he would have to earn a living. When he came back to the U.S., he was hired as a technician at Atari.

Wozniak moved into his own apartment in Cupertino and slowly adjusted to the workday world. Though he was a full-fledged adult and therefore "responsible," there was no way he would lose his prankish sense of humor. When he went with his friends to fast-food joints, he always berated the fare, sometimes adding the words "Alka-Seltzer, for your convenience" to the menu. At one called Bob's Big Boy, Woz put Fizrin, an antacid, in the sugar bowl. He patiently waited until an unsuspecting patron's coffee began to erupt like a restless volcano. When he attended a friend's high school graduation, he unfurled a huge banner bearing a middle-finger gesture to the class (he called it the "Brazilian good luck sign"). Well, nobody ever accused Woz of having impeccably good taste.

One of his more organized prankster efforts was his Dial-A-Joke Service. Though the concept wasn't exactly revolutionary, Woz's service was. He wasn't going to have any prissy nonoffensive Las Vegas–stand-up-comic-type humor. His would specialize in ethnic jokes. Since Woz was of Polish descent, he began in a self-deprecating mode. A caller would dial in and Woz's recorded voice would tell a fifteen-second Polish joke. His service became so popular that he eventually received around two thousand calls a day. People with similar phone numbers complained about wrong numbers, so Woz had to change the number several times. (It's still in existence, 408–435–5555.) When the Polish-American Congress threatened to sue him, he lampooned other ethnic backgrounds (Italian jokes became popular). Then he eventually combined origins, thinking he might as well offend many kinds of people at once. A typical joke went, "Did you hear the one about the man who was half-Italian and half-Polish? He made himself an offer he couldn't understand." And there was Woz cackling in the background. When he manned the phone in person, he used the name "Stanley Zeber Zenskanitsky."

Since Woz was fairly shy and spent most of his spare time with electronics, the Dial-A-Joke Service helped him meet women. He could listen to callers' voices, pick up the phone, and start a conversation if he wanted. One night a teen-ager named Alice Robertson called and Woz, finding the voice interesting, answered the phone and said, "I'll bet I can hang up faster than you can." He hung up. Alice's girl friend called back and got the two together again on the phone. They talked for a long while. Several calls later, in late December, 1973, Woz worked up the nerve to meet her. They began dating. Eventually, they got married. In a way, they were a typical young dual-career, high-tech couple. Woz worked at Hewlett-Packard, and Alice did microscopic welding for a defense industry–supported company. Alice knew of his affection for rodents, so she bought him some mice. Woz had such a fine touch with the critters that he didn't need to cage them. If he wanted to catch one to play with, he lightly crumpled a paper bag on the floor until one jumped in.

For Wozniak, Hewlett-Packard was a perfect place to be. Though it was a straitlaced firm in Palo Alto with a neatly tailored industrial-park image, it had refreshingly progressive policies, especially where creativity was involved. Indeed, H-P used many of the management techniques that have come to be identified with the Japanese style. An employee was free to use his workbench on his own time for personal projects. An engineer didn't need to wear a suit and tie. Allen Baum, for example, favored a T-shirt and a couple of flannel shirts for his work uniform. With his scraggly beard, he looked more like someone on his way to a peace demonstration than a guy who built computers. Woz went to work dressed casually, too.

Woz's desk abutted that of another calculator engineer, Stanley Mintz. Mintz remembers Woz's sense of playfulness right from his first days on the job. If Mintz had spent too much time talking, he would arrive at work and notice that the mouthpiece of his phone was taped. Woz knew how to drop a hint. Mintz was a licensed private pilot, and when Woz found out that he had screwed up a flight and missed a checkpoint, Woz placed a length of tape on his desk that led all the way to the men's room. He didn't want his companion to lose his way to the john. Most of all, Mintz remembers how smart Wozniak was. "I thought I was very good," he says. "I thought I was a great engineer until I met him. There's really no way to tell, but I would guess that Woz is one of the ten best, maybe the five best logic designers in the world."

When Woz finished work, he tinkered on his own. He also kept up with his other friends, like Steve Jobs. Jobs had access to the latest video games at Atari, so Woz, who became an incurable addict, would often get to play a new one while it was still in the test stage.

By 1974, the thought of small computers that electronic hobbyists could play with was beginning to pique the interest of businessmen. A company in New Mexico named MITS came up with an idea to sell a kit that enabled a person to assemble his own computer. They called it the Altair, and when it came to the attention of the editors of *Popular Electronics* magazine, they decided to put it on the cover of the January 1975 issue. The MITS people expected to sell perhaps eight hundred that year. When *Popular Electronics* came out, they immediately got orders for four hundred. Clearly, the hobbyist was ready and anxious to graduate from transistors. The ham radio freaks were about to be ushered into a new era. A number of folks in Silicon Valley heard about the Altair, and soon another firm named Imsai came out with a computer kit, too.

The corporate–big government image of the computer had officially begun to erode, though only a few seers knew it at the time. Soon there were unconventional—and certainly not very corporate—names emerging like The People's Computer Company and Kentucky Fried Computers.

An electronic proletariat was beginning to sprout.

One prime catalyst would be an unassuming engineer with a thick shock of white hair. His name was Gordon French. French was a computer systems designer, a man who had headed a team that installed a $5-million job for the Social Security Administration in Maryland. His firm was so pleased with his work for the administration that it wanted to move him permanently to the East Coast. "They wanted me to continue in government work, and they wanted me to move my family out there," he said. "But I said, 'No way. It's just impossible. I am not going to move there because the weather is just awful.'" Those words, spoken in true and sincere California style, indicated the kid in French's personality that seemed stuck in his corporate body. Fortunately, it was struggling to get loose.

French had written articles for obscure newsletters like *The Experimenter's Computer,* and he began making contacts with other computer hobbyists. A man named Carl Helmers saw his writing and called to chat. Helmers told French he wanted to start a small computer magazine named *Byte.* French told him it was a lousy name; call it anything but that. Helmers ignored his advice, as the saying goes, all the way to the bank. *Byte* would become the first "small-systems journal" and one day grow to *Vogue*-like prosperity in number of advertising pages. French also met a man named Fred Moore, who had bought the third or fourth Altair computer kit produced by MITS. Moore was the quintessential new-age technological flower child. He was a kind-hearted, gentle sort who was on the board of Stewart Brand's *Whole Earth Catalog.* The Whole Earth people were Moore's kind of people. Stewart Brand had a unique talent. He could wade through the technological quagmire and discover nonaggressive tools for common folks. One day in January 1975, French and Moore stumbled onto the street outside The People's Computer Company.

"Wouldn't it be nice if people who had their own computers could get together?" French asked Moore.

Moore nodded. When and where, he wanted to know? French suggested meeting in his garage in Menlo Park. Interested Silicon Valley engineers could talk about the latest in computers. Sort of an aviator's holiday, in a way. Imagine the Boeing 747 pilot who is pining for his day off. He is anxious to get behind the controls of a little Piper or Cessna so he can remember what real flying is like.

The same idea applied to computer engineers. Moore agreed to handle the publicity, and French would borrow the folding chairs. But Moore was always broke, so he had to ask French for five dollars to print some postcard-sized handbills, which Moore eventually tacked up on bulletin boards at Stanford University.

Allen Baum saw the notice and suggested that he and Steve Wozniak attend.

That apocalyptic first meeting of the Homebrew Computer Club was held on March 5, 1975. Twenty-one people showed up, including Woz and Baum and a guy named Lee Felsenstein. If anyone spoke the same technical dialect as French, Moore, Baum, and Wozniak—as well as shared the new-age sensibility—it was Felsenstein. As a kid Felsenstein had been precocious in the same vein as Wozniak. He won a prize at a science fair with a design of a satellite that transmitted signals to a radio. He admits he expected more acclaim for his invention. Felsenstein was a talented engineer, opinionated iconoclast, and the former "military editor" of the *Berkeley Barb,* a classic alternate newspaper of the sixties. He was also a leader in the 1965 antiwar march on the Oakland Army Terminal. If you'd met him at a peace demonstration, you'd have been surprised to learn what his profession was. Felsenstein became the club's informal master of ceremonies and set the group's anarchic political tone: no dues, no initiation fee, no membership application. The only thing the group agreed on was the need to keep meeting. The first computer shown was Moore's Altair. "It was grand," French says. "It had 256 bytes in it, no way of input and output. But we were able to turn it on and flip switches and consider that now the time had come when you could own your own computer."

After the first three meetings, the club's membership grew dramatically, so much that it needed a bigger space than French's garage. Eventually, the group secured access to an auditorium at the Stanford Linear Accelerator Center (SLAC). By the end of the year, some five hundred computer nuts were meeting on the second Wednesday of every month. Of course, the club still had "unofficial" status despite its immense popularity. Lee Felsenstein would open meetings by announcing, "Welcome to the Homebrew Computer Club which does not exist." Homebrew attracted not only the established Silicon Valley engineers but youngsters who were self-taught electronic enthusiasts, much as Wozniak had been ten years earlier. Steve Jobs began showing up, too. So did Captain Crunch, which gave some people the impression he was trying to outgrow his phone-freaking image. During the first part of the session, the "mapping" period, members would make announcements to swap or sell computers or bootleg parts thereof.

It was not uncommon for somebody to raise his hand and ask, "Is there anyone here from Intel?" When nobody acknowledged, the guy would say, relieved, "Okay, I've got some Intel chips I'd like to raffle off."

Then there would be demonstrations of new designs. And finally, there was a "random access" session, in which the members would break into small groups. The two most popular microprocessors—the microprocessor is the heart of most hobby computers—were the 6502 from MOS Technology and Intel's 8080. There were fans of both, and nobody cared that there was so little programming available for them.

In those days, computer programming for small machines consisted of Microsoft Basic 1.0. There were no floppy disks or even cassette tape-loaded machines. A programmer used punched paper tape, the slowest, most primitive, and most inexpensive method of coding information so a computer could understand it. One programmer got his machine to play the tune "Daisy," and he proudly demonstrated it on a transistor radio. He had used static memory, which was not permanent. When someone pulled out the plug, the tune was lost. He had to go through the long, tedious, and complicated chores of flipping switches to reprogram it. There were no real fully compact computers, consisting of the central processing unit, keyboard, and monitor. Usually, members brought a TV set to hook up to their machines.

Homebrew meetings were important for one other thing: professional contacts. Anyone seriously considering starting a computer company had a veritable fount of talent to choose from. It wasn't long before a group of people decided to start Processor Technology, a company that would build a small computer. The unit was designed by Lee Felsenstein and named Sol, in honor of Les Solomon, the technical editor of *Popular Electronics*. It was a modest firm with humble beginnings. The blueprint for the Sol was tacked to a wall. When Gordon French saw the size of the operation—the shipping bay was no bigger than his living room—he knew he had found a new home. He precipitously quit his job and even took a five-hundred-dollar a week pay cut. Processor Tech needed him; he was the only guy around with any sheet-metal experience, and someone had to screw the thing together. Later, Lee Felsenstein gave him credit for "realizing" the design, a term he thought appropriately confusing yet satisifying.

Thus the club saw the first of many start-up companies; in a way, it was the birthplace of the home-computer business. Nobody knew it at the time, but Homebrew was to foment a multi-billion-dollar industry. The first two dozen people who met in Gordon French's garage formed some twenty-one different firms among them—companies like Apcose, Cromemco, North Star. According to French's calculations, "Three have gone belly-up, two have been purchased by larger organizations, and the balance are still in business. Not a bad batting average." Later, of course, other members would start ancillary businesses like *Byte* magazine, the West Coast Computer Faire (the first successful small-computer trade show), and the Byte Shop chain of computer retail stores. The first portable home computer, the Osborne I, was also originated by a casual member, Adam Osborne.

But the biggest success story emanating from Homebrew was that of Steve Wozniak and Steve Jobs. They were going to begin Apple Computer Inc.

Chapter Seven

Selling Apples at the Filling Station

Steve Wozniak saw all the computers at the Homebrew Club meetings, and knew that it was time to work on his own design. The gatherings were attracting a lot of smart engineers, and smart engineers had substantial egos. Anybody with minimal talent could put together a "kludge" (pronounced "klooje"), a sloppy design with wires trailing from every port. The object was to show off, to see who could build a cleaner, cleverer, and more esthetic computer. Woz was, of course, a show-off, and this was one place where it was socially acceptable— indeed, almost a requirement—to show off.

At Hewlett-Packard Woz was getting bored working on calculators. He already knew all there was to know about them. Company engineers were gearing up to work on a programmable terminal, a new desktop computer, and when Woz heard about it he begged to get on the design team. He just wanted to be part of the project in any way; printer interface boards, writing software, anything. He was turned down. He couldn't understand why. "They said I didn't have enough education," Wozniak remembers. "But I had the knowledge. I could teach myself. I never had a course in school in any of the projects I ever worked on at Hewlett-Packard." Still, Woz was not the kind of person who complained and got cranky. Instead, he decided to build a computer on his own. "Some day, I wanted to have a minicomputer like Data General's Nova," he said. "Some day, I wanted to own my own, and it might even have 4K in it [an amount of memory capacity roughly equal to seven hundred words of text]." He would compete with his own company, though he never viewed it that way because basically he's a noncompetitive guy.

There was only one small problem. Wozniak didn't know anything about the current microcomputer technology. "I didn't know what an Altair 8800 was," he said, referring to an early-model computer. "I knew about minicomputers [small business machines]. I didn't even know the numbers on the microprocessors. I remember that Gordon French was very interested in the 8080, and he had demonstrated it in his garage. He thought there was a big future in that machine. He passed out data sheets for it. I took the sheet home at night and read it thoroughly. I pored over it, and I realized this was a minicomputer. Hey, I thought. These microprocessors are doing the same things. That was my starting point." All he had to do was translate his thinking from minis to micros: the instruction sets, the input-output configuration, and all the other myriad details. He had read through dozens of minicomputer manuals. It wouldn't be difficult at all. He just had to think smaller.

He worked after hours and at night and assembled a small printed circuit board using the 6502 microprocessor. When he was finished, he planned to take it to a Homebrew meeting to show his friends.

Meanwhile, the Homebrew meetings had become what one member called "an IC cracker barrel," meaning that an engineer could catch up on all the latest gossip in Silicon Valley regarding integrated circuits and the like. Fred Moore edited the group's newsletter, and Gordon French was the unofficial software librarian. Members could borrow any tape they wanted from

French, as long as they returned two copies. The theory was, Let's keep expanding the library. It wasn't that convenient, either. Remember, you had to toggle a bunch of switches and wait for ten minutes or more while a paper tape program was loading.

Another member, Jim Warren, recalls the special metabolic nature of the Homebrew meetings. He feels the club attracted an unusual number of what he calls "space-case" engineers—technophiles who were innovative and creative and found the corporate atmosphere stifling. French and Wozniak were beginning to fit that definition. Warren himself was something of a generational maverick. He had been a confirmed academic, armed with bachelor's and master's degrees in math. He taught and had a successful second career as a consultant for a number of highly respected electronics firms. Also, he loved to play with circuit boards. Through Homebrew, his life began to change. He would eventually throw the first big computer show, the West Coast Computer Faire in San Francisco, which attracted thirteen thousand people in April 1977. Today, the transformation looks complete. The academic has given way to the entrepreneur. Warren lives in a large, beautifully crafted wooden home atop a mountain in Woodside. Each morning, his house is enveloped by the morning fog, and it is often cool, even in summer, until the sun burns through the haze. Warren is a bear of a fellow with a substantial beard and an equally substantial girth. He prefers to work in a T-shirt and warms his fanny using a wood-burning stove.

Warren does not remember the introduction of Wozniak's computer as being anything spectacular, though he concedes that it received a warm reception. Woz got up in front of the crowd in the SLAC auditorium and held up his invention. He explained what was on the printed circuit board, how many chips were in it, and so on. "This was in the days before you had to think about how you were going to introduce a product," recalls Wozniak. "It was just, more or less, a board." There was no case on it, naturally, because the idea was to see what was inside. It was a nice little innovation, says Warren, clean and simple and physically neat. It was not exotic. He does not recall there being any technological breakthrough. "But it was a step up from the hobby stage," Warren says. He and some of his friends were very disappointed that Woz had not used the S−100 bus, however. A "bus" is a type of lead or pin connector on a printed circuit board. Since most computers use more than one board—indeed, in those days they needed several to do anything worthwhile—the boards must be hooked together. Woz's design precluded using any S-100 bus boards, and several Homebrew members were partial to that system because it was so inexpensive and widely available. This was a minor objection, of course, and not an entirely accurate one. Woz had used the 6502 microprocessor because you could buy one for twenty dollars. The 8080 that was so popular cost a few hundred. Woz based his microprocessor choice on one factor: the low cost. Eventually, these hobbyist differences would exemplify a widespread future industry problem now denoted with the catchword "compatibility." (Or, why software for an Atari, for example, won't work in an IBM PC or any other type of computer.)

No, Jim Warren wasn't very impressed with Woz's computer. But something else about it did overwhelm him. When he learned that Woz had designed both the hardware (the computer) and software (the instruction sets that told it what to do) in his *spare time* while holding a full-time job at H-P, he was amazed.

About this time in 1975, Adam Osborne made one of his three appearances at a Homebrew meeting. He was a corporate type, a chemical engineering Ph.D. who had worked for Shell Oil and was earning a living as a technical writer. Born in Thailand, he was the son of a British diplomat and one of the foppier people in the audience. He wore three-piece suits, while everyone else wore jeans. He was brash and opinionated. He thought there might be a market for a book aimed at computer hobbyists, so he wrote one of the first available, called *Introduction to Microcomputers*. It wasn't a book in the sense of a narrative discussion. Rather, it was a listings manual. It discussed programming and was densely illustrated with circuit diagrams. He published it himself.

Adam Osborne remembers sitting next to Wozniak

and Jobs and looking at Woz's early computer sketches. "He must have been really broke," Osborne recalls. "He didn't even have any drafting paper."

Gordon French says that Osborne actually brought his books to Homebrew meetings looking to sell them. "Osborne came down there with a cardboard box of books, the one on how to program an 8080," French says. "We didn't know we weren't supposed to conduct business at these meetings." It was against the rules at Stanford.

Woz was happy with his computer design, but Steve Jobs was ecstatic about it. Why not sell it? He thought they should go into business. Woz wasn't interested. Jobs kept prodding him. He would take care of the business end, and Woz could deal with manufacturing. Why, they'd make a great team, just like in the old blue-box days.

Woz agreed, but unwillingly. Probably, he was in a pranksteresque mood, one in which he could humor his buddy Steve Jobs. Woz was smart enough to realize that building, marketing, and selling a computer was quite a great deal more complicated than purveying phone boxes door-to-door in college dorms.

Okay, the two would sell computers.

But right away there was a problem. Woz was a loyal employee, and he had done some of the circuit design at H-P, meaning on the company's workbench. He had daydreamed the design on H-P time, so he had an obligation to the company. What if H-P wanted to build it? He took the design to his supervisor. There was nothing really wrong with it, he was told. It was actually pretty nifty. But it wasn't something that fit in with the company's product line. On three separate occasions, Woz tried to interest Hewlett-Packard in his microcomputer. He was turned down each time. They weren't interested in the hobby market. Even if they built Woz's computer, and even if it was a successful product, it might cut into the sales of H-P's already well known and proven business machines. Undaunted, Woz asked the company for a legal release. His schematic was sent to all the appropriate departments, and in three days, the right to build and sell it was all his. Woz was impressed with how efficient the firm was.

Not a single hassle or a grunt from an overprotective lawyer. Woz was impressed with the minimal amount of red tape.

Since Jobs was a fruitarian at the time—he had worked in an apple orchard—they decided to call the machine the Apple. When they told Homebrew people they were going into business, everyone laughed, especially Gordon French. Nobody called a computer an Apple! Lee Felsenstein shook his head skeptically. He was already working for Processor Technology and his machine was almost ready for shipping. Wozniak was in earnest, Felsenstein thought. He said to himself, "If he fails, he's gonna fail big." He did sort of envy their guts. Here were two kids, somewhere between naive and blind, going into business and not knowing the first thing about it. Anyway, it was hardly a finished, refined product. It wasn't even in a box. It would be like selling a car without the wheels and transmission and brakes. Just the engine and no hood. That was all right with Wozniak; everyone would see how good his engine was.

First, they needed investment capital. Jobs had an old VW microbus and Wozniak had a fancy H-P calculator. They sold them both and raised around thirteen hundred dollars. Jobs could ride his bicycle around Silicon Valley, and Woz would have to borrow a calculator or do his arithmetic work by hand. They needed a space to work. Jobs commandeered his family garage. If it was okay for Hewlett and Packard to start in a garage, it was okay for Woz and Jobs. The two cleared out the junk and stored it in John McCollum's electronic shop at the high school. Next, they needed people to buy the damn thing. Orders. And once they had orders, they had to get parts. Woz certainly wasn't going to cadge computer chips from Fairchild any more.

Paul Terrell, who had gone to Homebrew meetings, had opened one of the first retail outlets, a Byte Shop, in Mountain View, and sensed the hobbyists' demand for computers. He had been selling the Altair and Imsai, and soon would be carrying Processor Technology's machine. In those days, he sold "kit insurance." If you paid an extra $50 for the kit, he guaranteed it would work. (He had a bench in the back of the store with all the usual testing scopes. One of the beauties of this technology was that there was little in the way of moving parts. A chip could be defective, but a good one wouldn't wear out that easily. And a computer was 90 percent modular. If a chip was bad, simply pop out the old one and put in a new one.) Wozniak had brought in his prototype, and Terrell was impressed. "It was real state of the art," he said, even though it didn't yet have a power supply, or a keyboard, or even a case. Jobs asked him how many he wanted. Terrell gave the two an order for fifty boards, if they could be delivered in a month. Jobs said, no problem. Woz and Jobs would charge Terrell $549.00 for each unit, and the store would sell them for $666.66, approximately a $100.00 markup.

"They took my purchase order with them and they started shopping for a parts supplier to give them thirty days credit," Terrell says.

Wozniak and Jobs didn't exactly fit the image of refined businessmen. They went around the valley in T-shirts and jeans. Woz wore sneakers or boots; Jobs preferred sandals. It wasn't long before Terrell was interrupted by a phone call at a local meeting of the electrical engineers association. The caller was from Kramer Electronics.

"I've got these two hippie-type characters here with your purchase order," the caller said. "Is it bona fide?"

"Yeah," Terrell replied, somewhat sheepishly, wondering whether he'd ever see a Wozniak-Jobs computer.

The two Steves began working feverishly in the garage, assembling the boards by hand. Over the bench was their inspiration, a "Star Trek" poster of Mr. Spock. Thinking "logically" seemed to define what computers were about. Woz soldered circuits faster than he ever had before. By the end of the month, they were exhausted. They delivered their first computers to Terrell's store.

What ensued is in some historical dispute. Terrell claims that they only completed twenty boards at first. Wozniak insists that they delivered all fifty, but since their deal was for cash on delivery, Terrell partially reneged because he could only pay enough for half. He would have to pay the remainder of the bill when he sold a few. (In those days, it wasn't uncommon for a store to ask a customer for a 50 percent deposit, which

Terrell often did. And, of course, nobody did any kind of business without at least some fast talking to get credit.) Terrell's cash-flow problem apparently enraged Steve Jobs because they needed money to buy more parts. Wozniak, however, was calm about it. It was a money matter, and Woz didn't become unglued over money, much less any other crisis. His computer was going to be sold to hobbyists, and at a price that was affordable. People would soon be using a computer with his name on it. There was much more ego gratification attached to that than money could buy.

Either way, Paul Terrell says he saw there were some H-P parts in it, and he remembers that he thought, "I better put a case on it." Wozniak had not yet written much in the way of software. There was no integer BASIC for the 6502 microprocessor at the time. But there was for the 8080 microprocessor. A hobbyist at this time could still do more with someone else's machine. Terrell remembers it as "very basic BASIC." It could do "LIST" and "RUN" and only about four or five other instructions.

During 1975–76, the time that Jobs and Wozniak built those first computers (then called just the "Apple" and now known as the Apple I), their business didn't exactly flourish. Only about 175 computers were sold. Luckily, a couple of Homebrew people decided to purchase one after Jobs extolled its superiority at meetings. Jobs and Woz would sit in the back of SLAC's auditorium, way up by the projection booth near the center section of chairs, and repeatedly hold court about the machine. Mostly, it was Jobs who spoke. Woz only talked a few times. "Jobs was the front man, the promoter, or whatever you want to call him," Gordon French says. Jim Warren is even more blunt: "Woz was the quiet, technically competent one, and Jobs was the volatile one who said, 'You've got to see this computer, the Apple. We're going to market it.'"

Of course, after Adam Osborne's faux pas with his makeshift bookstall, there was no way Woz and Jobs would get away with selling the Apple at Homebrew meetings. They could arrange a sale at SLAC, but they had to consummate it somewhere else. It is amusing to think that dealing computers at Stanford had the same sort of hush-hush appearance as dealing illegal drugs. The underground supermarket, however, was not too far from the university. After the meetings, the gadgeteers would meet at the Shell gas station in Sharon Heights and conduct business. Recalls Gordon French, "We would first adjourn from SLAC down to the gas station, trade chips and parts, buy your Apple I, or whatever. Then we adjourned to another place, a bar called the Oasis. At that point, we would swap trade secrets. Some of this was kind of testy. You didn't dare give away the company store. But you could irritate your competitors by bragging or needling them. You know, 'I've got this new computer under way, and we're going to be out by September, and we're just going to blow everybody away.' There was lots of misinformation given out at the Oasis. You tried to mislead as many people as you possibly could. There were only a few companies. All of us were now in business, so the whole idea was mislead the guy sitting next to you."

French laughs, thinking that it was at Homebrew meetings that the microcomputer transition began to occur. At first, the meetings were quiet and cordial and communal. There was a freshness, an openness in sharing information. Then, when the membership began splitting off into various factions, under the aegis of new company names, the game got more serious, bigger and faster and more competitive. "We were always afraid we were going to get co-opted by IBM," said Lee Felsenstein. "We were like a tiny band of outlaws." And naturally his worst fear was not unfounded.

What happened? Simple technological progress. What started as a hobby became a business. And the business was about to turn into a full-fledged industry, replete with venture-capital firms, Wall Street analysts, and stock offerings. These prople weren't co-opted by IBM, but they did sell out. Gordon French, lounging in his modest Sunnyvale studio apartment, reminisced about the early days, the mid-seventies, which illustrates just how fast the computer industry moves. Next to his bed he keeps a framed photo of himself in which his hair runs to shoulder length. Today, French has a pile of computers and printers in his living room, including a collector's item, the Processor Technology Sol. He fondly remembers sipping champagne on the loading dock when the first 250 machines were ready for shipment. The company is no longer in business. Today French has a small business making cardboard casings for floppy disks, the software packages now standard with most small computers. He shrugs. He doesn't seem to mind that he never got rich from his hobby. Gordon likes to say he has a contempt for money matched only by Steve Wozniak.

Co-opted? Nobody can say for certain. Some people were, and some weren't. Either way, the stakes undoubtedly had escalated.

Lee Felsenstein recalls making a trip to Atlantic City for a computer hobby show on Labor Day weekend in 1976. He just happened to be sitting near Wozniak and Jobs on the airplane. "They were sitting next to each other holding a little plywood box with their computer in it," Felenstein said. "I forget who held it; I think it was in Jobs's lap. I remember thinking it was the epitome of a tiny company. All the employees and its entire product were on two seats of the plane."

Chapter Eight

The Apple II Is Born

Steve Jobs was intently pursuing the idea of making the Apple computer a big-time product. He had talked to enough people who felt that the machine was good, but it wasn't quite finished. By "finished," Jobs thought they meant complete in the sense of a consumer product. It had to do more, he felt, than add and subtract and run little musical tunes. It had to be useful. It had to draw pictures. It had to balance your checkbook and catalogue your recipes. Someday, it should be able to open your garage door or adjust your thermostat or turn the house lights on and off and adjust the thermostat while you were on vacation. It had to be dazzling. It had to be packaged and marketed and sold like, well, toothpaste. We were on the eve of a revolution. If Henry Ford could put a car in every garage, why, Steve Jobs would put a computer in every living room. Jobs had a vision. And that was that the home computer would become a great home appliance, nothing short of a necessity. Other people also had this vision, but they kept it to themselves. Jobs told everyone he met. He was obsessive about this.

Steve Wozniak was not. He wanted his computer to be fun, even useful, but as for doing a Procter and Gamble routine... well, no way. He had a respectable job; he didn't have to sing for his supper. Woz was a true hacker. Computer chips were like little jewels, and when you put them together the result was just beautiful and clean and esthetic. The finished product was like a necklace, classy and understated. Not gaudy. A computer's innards were something to ogle and marvel at.

Jobs said the Apple should be improved and updated, and Woz did at least agree with this. They had plenty of competition from Processor Technology's Sol alone. Since their enterprise was not yet thriving, Woz didn't quit his job at Hewlett-Packard. He decided to work on the new design at night, which was when he did his best thinking anyway. At dinner at his parents' home, he sometimes talked about his new project with his father. The Wozniak kitchen counter, in a way, was the first boardroom for Apple. When Steve Jobs thought the new version should have some additional function, he would tell Woz, and Woz would think about it. If Woz balked, Jobs would appeal to his father. Sometimes Woz worked in his own apartment, other times on his parents' living room floor. He often liked to work lying down. Strange as it seems, much of the Apple computer was designed while Woz was in the prone position.

Jerry Wozniak saw that his son was charged up with a huge burst of potential energy, waiting to be unleashed. He knew that when Steve went into his design-combat mode, nothing else mattered. He would not even look outside to check the weather. The rest of his life was abruptly put on hold. He routinely forgot about paying the rent or any of his bills. Woz's brother Mark was incredulous. Woz had regressed into a slob stage. "You can't imagine what his apartment looked like," Mark says. "It was disgusting, really disgusting. Papers all over the place, rotted food, and garbage overflowing." Woz's father, however, didn't care that his son wasn't so neat. At least he was working on something substantial. He was *applying* himself.

"The first year, 1976, was the most interesting year at Apple," Jerry Wozniak says, "when Steve was in his apartment and Jobs was in his garage. You heard all these ideas. Everything that's in the Apple IIe now [the company's newer version of its flagship product] was discussed back then. They had already talked to companies about making very complicated chips."

What Wozniak remembers most is going back to his workbench at H-P at all kinds of crazy hours, 2:00 and 3:00 A.M. "The people at Hewlett-Packard who know me best," he likes to say, "are the night security guards." (He does allow that he did filch a lot of time from Hewlett-Packard.) His wife Alice worked a different shift, and they soon became ships passing in the night. They saw each other less and less. It wasn't a good time for Woz to be married, his mother remembers. Her son was in love with a computer. "I don't think he spent much time at the marriage," Margaret Wozniak says. Woz's loyal friends defend Woz, however. They say that Alice didn't spend much time at it either.

Apple Computer needed a printed advertisement. Jobs and Woz convinced another friend, Ron Wayne, to do an ink drawing that would evoke the company image. The original logo showed Isaac Newton sitting under a tree, an apple about to fall on his head (gravity at work, one supposes), with a little banner that bore the name Apple Computer. A caption under the illustration read, "A mind forever voyaging through strange seas of thought...alone." That accurately described Wozniak's preferred work habits. Woz liked the ad because it evoked the new-age mentality of friendly, noncorporate computers. It looked more appropriate for *Mother Earth News* than for *Popular Mechanics*. "It was sort of neat that you could get anybody to do something that took more than three minutes to draw, like our computer logo," Woz says. "For the product we had, I didn't think you should do more than draw a cartoon." Ron Wayne was given 10 percent of the company for his work from day one (he also laid out printed circuit boards). Wayne even typed up the legal documents that made the three partners.

Wayne was also supposed to give the two Steves busi-

ness advice. But he didn't have much confidence in them. After all, they weren't exactly paying him a full-time salary. He wanted out. Woz and Jobs bought back his interest for eight hundred dollars cash. When Wozniak tells people about this, listeners shake their heads in disbelief. Wayne gave up a piece of stock worth millions. But Wozniak shrugs and smiles. He feels Wayne made a business decision that was sound at the time.

It took Wozniak the better part of a year to design the improved version of his computer, which would be dubbed the Apple II. Inside, Wozniak had created...

small masterpiece. It really took an engineer to...

ciate what he had done. Most of the othe...

puters needed a whole series of add...

them to work. Woz's computer h...

"mother board," with six...

used double the num...

did twice as m...

the hardw...

too. T...

wa...

thin...

himsel...

Steve Job...

Woz and...

on the future o...

still working in a...

a hell of a lot abou...

sive as Woz, an incu...

suit was in his salesman...

game, and you could only...

eye to eye

g, they were

s didn't know

was as compul-

c. But his strong

erely talked a good

for so long. Sooner or

later, you had to deliver. And ow they didn't even have Ron Wayne to advise them. Though Woz had a new computer, he had designed it mostly for himself and wasn't comfortable with the idea of commercializing it. "I wasn't sure whether I wanted it to be a product at all," he admits. "It was pretty much just designed to show my friends. You bet I didn't want a case. Nobody could count the number of chips. Steve [Jobs] was thinking in terms of a big product, a big move for the company. He was handling all the marketing himself. And although he couldn't sell many Apple I's, he knew there was a market for thousands of a big computer. This was based on the fact that he was in contact with the dealers, and they were selling the Sol computer [Processor Tech's] very heavily. And that was the closest in the Apple direction. It had a keyboard standard, video standard, a certain amount of memory standard. The Sol was the closest thing to the Apple II. It was kind of a step in between the Apple I and the Apple II."

It was left to Jobs to look for investment capital. Jobs asked nearly everyone he knew for help. He called up Nolan Bushnell, his high-tech business idol, over at Atari. Bushnell had the same lukewarm reaction that H-P had had when it was approached by Woz. One East Coast dealer at the time, Stan Veit, was on a business trip in Silicon Valley. Veit had opened the first retail outlet in New York City that sold more than one brand of microcomputer. When Jobs bumped into him, he told him about the Apple II. Just one minute, Jobs said. I'll bring it right over. Jobs went home, put the computer (with a TV set) into the basket of his bicycle, and pedaled over to where Veit was staying. Woz and Jobs gave him the digital demo, and Veit liked the computer.

Then Jobs said, "We'd like you to invest in the company." The offer was simple because Apple was desperate. Give us ten thousand dollars and we'll give you 10 percent of the company, Jobs told Veit. Veit graciously declined, with a woeful tale of cash-flow problems in his store. If he had ten thousand dollars, he said, he'd put it in his own business. (Early on, the two Steves did borrow five thousand dollars from Allen Baum's father, but it was a straight loan which they repaid in full.)

Jobs wanted to do a heavy advertising and promotion campaign, too. "Steve really fell in love with an ad that said 'Little Johnny gets a computer,' or something," Wozniak recalls. "A little kid is holding up an Intel PC [printed circuit] board. It seemed so ridiculous to us technical sorts. But Steve loved it. He thought it was the greatest ad ever done." Jobs investigated, and discovered that the ad was produced by Regis McKenna, Silicon Valley's most prestigious high-tech public relations agency. McKenna was handling Intel, and he had recently taken on the Byte Shop retail outlets. Regis's company was growing quite rapidly, and he didn't need the business. McKenna told Jobs he was too expensive—and anyway, he wasn't much interested in doing business with a guy in his early twenties who wore his hair to his shoulders and had a beard that made him resemble Fidel Castro.

It was clear that Steve Jobs's ambition at this point far outstripped his perception of reality, and his ability. But he was so confident and arrogant and naive that he kept trying. He was pumped up. He got an answering service for the company to help display a facade of professionalism. If a dealer or supplier called Apple, the service connected the caller to Jobs's stepparents' home. Jobs hustled so hard that his parents could rarely make a personal phone call without first making a reservation.

Woz and Jobs finally admitted to themselves that neither of them was qualified to actually run a company. Not only did they need investment capital, they needed an experienced manager, a man they could call president of Apple. One by one, qualified applicants heard the word and showed up at Jobs's garage door. Everyone was given an immediate interview. One guy made them feel very bush league and ended up interviewing them. He asked them business questions like, "Where's the value added?" and "Who do you think the market is?" Jobs and Wozniak felt like beginners. They couldn't fool this guy.

"We didn't know any professional marketing words," Wozniak says, almost apologetically. "We didn't know how to describe various markets. So my answer was along the lines of, 'There are a million ham radio operators in the country, and computers are bigger than ham radios now. So the market's more than a million. It's valid for the hobbyists alone.' But it didn't turn him on, and the way we presented it there was no way we could get further interest on his part." But that man did do the two Steves a favor. He knew a young and successful millionaire who might help them out. He had once worked for Intel and was now looking for something challenging to do. His name was Mike Markkula. He'd see if he was interested.

Markkula eventually decided to investigate these two youngsters with the Apple II computer. Jobs and Wozniak, mostly Jobs, went through the spiel. Markkula thought it was a pretty good product and had a lot of potential. He offered to invest some of his own money in it. But first he wanted a full-time commitment from Wozniak. Woz was still working for H-P, and Markkula realized immediately that there was still a lot of important hardware and software deisgn work to be done in order for the product, and ultimately the company, to make it. He knew that it was too much to handle even for a first-class engineer in his spare time. He had one other important stipulation. He was more interested in doing the creative business work—obtaining bank financing and so on. After the company was up and running, he didn't want to do the day-to-day supervisory work. So eventually, they would also need to bring in another manager. A corporation would have to be formed. Markkula said he wanted a 20 percent share of the new venture; the two Steves would each have 26 percent. The remaining stock would be sold to other investors rounded up by Markkula.

But Markklula was getting ahead of himself. He had erroneously assumed that Wozniak would rush out the door and immediately give notice. Woz, of course, had a nice secure job at Hewlett-Packard, earning around eighteen thousand a year. He wasn't sure he wanted to give it up just to go into business, especially one that was so risky. Woz balked. Markkula was insistent. He wouldn't get involved unless he had Wozniak full time.

Woz gave it some more thought and said no. He was unconvinced. Perhaps Ron Wayne was right after all. Maybe they were in over their heads. Why ruin a good thing by doing something commercial with it? Meanwhile, Jobs, because he was an adopted son, had spent a lot of time at the Wozniak household. Jerry Wozniak had become a kind of confidante, fulfilling an almost father-like role. Jobs appealed to Woz's father, hoping he could influence his son. He even called up Wozniak's friends, badgering them to convince Woz to go into business. Woz says Jobs actually cried about his decision. One Homebrew member said, "Woz didn't want to start a computer company. He just wanted to design boards for Hewlett-Packard. Jobs would say, 'I've been talking to Woz, and I just can't get through to him. Can you do something about it?'" That attitude typifies Jobs's unsubtle means of persuasion and his aggressive, go-after-it personality.

Woz finally changed his mind when he convinced himself that the Apple computer could indeed become a real product.

Markkula wondered if his investment might rely too much on Wozniak. "By the time I finally got talked into it, Mike decided he wanted 26 percent," Wozniak said. "I didn't think about percentages of ownership of a company. Money meant nothing to me anyway. But now, looking back, I realize why he and Steve at least wanted 52 percent." Wozniak giggles and smiles when he recalls this. "My action was a little too unpredictable, I guess. There was never any discussion about it. Now, I can totally understand it. Then, I couldn't. I could never understand why 52 percent of anything could matter anyway."

You have to marvel at the wonderful Wozniak naiveté. Here was a guy who got 800 on the College Boards math exam, wrote complex software, designed calculators, built computers in his *spare* time, and it never dawned on him that Jobs and Markkula had the controlling interest and future of Apple—soon to be Apple Computer Inc.—in their grip.

Mike Markkula told the two Steves that the first thing they needed was a plan, a formal business proposal. Since he had intimate knowledge about how plans were done, he'd start with that. Woz's father still has a good laugh over the business plan. "They wanted to be a five-hundred-million-dollar company in five years.

I thought. 'How naive can you be?' They were working out of a garage."

Steve Wozniak was twenty-five years old, and Jobs was all of twenty-one.

Chapter Nine

That First Go-Go Year

About a year earlier, just before Christmas in 1975, Steve Wozniak had met another youngster, Randy Wigginton, who was developing a robust interest in computers. They were introduced at a Homebrew meeting. Wigginton wasn't yet old enough to drive, so he asked Woz for rides home. Wigginton, who is slight and blond and good-looking in a way you might call "California healthy," liked Woz right away. He was going to Homestead High, and yes, he had some electronics courses with good old Mr. McCollum. His style of dress was typically West Coast casual: "Save the River" T-shirt, jeans, and sandals. You might have taken him for a surf bum. He was hungry to learn about digital design theory, and Woz seemed to know everything. After Homebrew meetings, the two would go to a fast-food restaurant and wolf down hamburgers, and Wigginton would ask questions. "I got my computer education at Denny's," he likes to say. Like Woz, he was mostly self-taught. He loved Woz's Apple computer design, and he eventually learned how to program one.

Wozniak had always kept in touch with Wigginton,

and now that Apple was a serious company, it was looking for help. Wigginton had become an accomplished 6502 programmer; he could write the complex instructions to tell the Apple what to do. Wozniak asked him to join the company. He was just sixteen years old. Wigginton was flattered, but knew his parents wouldn't exactly approve of his dropping out of high school to write computer programs. No matter. The company would accommodate to his education. As Apple Computer's first programmer, Wigginton worked from 4:00 to 8:00 A.M. and 3:00 to 8:00 P.M. and also on weekends. It seemed like a grueling schedule. Wigginton didn't care. It was more like full-time play than a full-time job. Right away, he noticed the disparate personalities of the two Steves. His hacker friend Woz was laid back and relaxed and always looking to play a joke. Jobs was serious, all business, and concerned himself with the most ridiculously small details. They all had badges with numbers that designated their seniority. Woz was number one, Jobs was number two, and Markkula was number three (Wigginton was number six). "Jobs nearly cried about the fact that Woz was number one," Wigginton says. "I swear, he wanted to be number zero. He was really upset about it."

Woz and Jobs also needed all sorts of technical help, so they paid a visit to Gordon French, who had suddenly quit Processor Technology. It was December 17, 1976. French says, "The two Steves came to me and Woz was particularly animated, I guess that's a reasonable way to describe it. They had spread this computer out. Now, we're talking about a circuit board with wires that led from one place to another. The power supply was in a cigar box. They brought a TV set to use as a monitor. Now, Woz is a very fast talker; he was talking like 1200-baud [a typical modem speed] all the time, going through what this thing could do. I must say that I was singularly unimpressed. I didn't like the 6502, and as a consequence, Jobs got a little salty with me. On the way out, Jobs asked, 'How many orders for Sols has Processor Tech got?' I said, '250.' And he said, 'That many?' That gives you some indication of what we thought was the market size."

Jobs, of course, knew that the Apple II computer

would not only have to work like a consumer product; it would have to look like one. This was where his real contribution to the company, perhaps his ingenious foresight, came in. Let his partner worry about what was inside the computer, he'd worry about the outside. After all, Woz wasn't going to.

Steve Jobs toyed with two kinds of drawings for a computer case. One that was not used had a little door, like a rolltop desk, that closed over the keyboard. Jobs felt that the computer still had a strong stigma. Suppose ordinary people, nonhackers, didn't want their friends to notice it in their living rooms? Eventually, he rejected that design. If he worried about the concept of the computer's acceptance to that extent, then his whole theory wasn't worth anything.

The important thing, he knew, was that it should not constantly remind people that it was a computer. The power supply shouldn't hum. No noisy fan either. The case should look flat, like a high-tech typewriter with the carriage cut off. He wanted it to shut from the bottom, so the screws wouldn't be an eyesore. He wanted it to be a light cream color. The case would definitely not be metal; injection-molded plastic was just as strong and lightweight. The central processing unit would weigh in at less than twelve pounds. In fact, Jobs was a little worried that it might be too light. He considered adding sash weights to the case so that when a customer lifted it, he would feel he was getting something substantial, his money's worth. Jobs was thinking like a new-car salesman. If the guy slams the door and it doesn't sound right, he won't buy it. He eventually rejected the weight idea.

Markkula's investment allowed Apple to look for legitimate factory space, and they found some in a small industrial facility in Cupertino, a community of thirty-eight thousand. Markkula asked Gordon French down to the company's new headquarters to talk him into working for them. It didn't look like a promising operation at all, French thought. Woz wanted him to "write an explanation of how to convert this thing from 16K RAM [random access memory] to 32K by saying you unplug this ROM [read only memory] and you cut that trace and so on." Woz and French had coffee across the street. French said he'd think about the offer. Then he went home and remembered that Woz's desk was right in the factory, and there were no closed offices; the workshop was in a corner. Finally, French said no. "When you see a computer company contained in less than eleven hundred square feet, it doesn't look that promising," he said. He had just quit Processor Technology over a disagreement with its management, yet Apple just wasn't enticing enough. Perhaps the dreamers of Homebrew were just dreamers? Maybe a people's computer wouldn't fly after all?

Steve Jobs still wanted a prestige promotional campaign, so he kept after Regis McKenna. For some time, Silicon Valley cognoscenti had heard that Regis McKenna had three times turned down Apple as a client. McKenna's version was published in *InfoWorld* magazine. He said, "Steve likes to tell that story. I think we had some disagreements on the marketing aspect of things. Steve was very persistent, as he is in everything. But I'm sure a lot of people turned Apple down in the early stages. Steve overcomes that by calling you at home all night long."

More likely, when McKenna found out that Markkula was on board, he decided to take on the Apple account. At least the bills had a reasonable chance of being paid. The first thing McKenna wanted to do was change the name of the computer. Apple sounded too rinky-dink. Nobody would buy it. It had to have a high-tech, serious name to go along with the look. Jobs and Woz said no. Another time, the two almost gave in and changed it. Jobs told everyone in the company that five o'clock that afternoon was the deadline to come up with a better name. If not, Apple stayed. Nobody could.

One of McKenna's first ads featured a color illustration of a typical family scene, showing the father using the computer to work on the household budget and the mother using it to store her recipes. It showed how little anyone knew at the time about who the potential buyer was. Now, Wozniak shakes his head as if to say, "How could we have been so stupid? Nobody buys a computer to do those things." Hindsight has given him a clear perspective on what has proven to be a somewhat accidental success. He says, "The circuitry of the computer defined the market, and not the product features. Oddly enough, the design came out very well, even though the product didn't define the market. Thank God, there was no market at the time." What he means is that if the product had tried to cater to their idea of a market, they wouldn't have figured out how to build it. This is Woz's interpretation of what envious competitors refer to when they insist Apple simply got lucky.

Randy Wigginton was Wozniak's main assistant in software. He spent a lot of time debugging Woz's code. That meant that when Woz wrote a long, complicated program, and it didn't quite work correctly, he had to wade through it, line by line, to see where his boss had made a mistake. The process is detailed and often boring, but Randy didn't mind because he was still learning. Anyway, Woz was too busy to debug his own programs.

The company was tiny, of course, and Markkula himself had to help out with the chores. He knew that to touch the neophyte consumer, to go beyond the hobbyist, he had to develop useful, easy-to-implement software. He and Wigginton wrote the checkbook program, which, according to Wigginton, "was like the only applications program we sold for years." Working late into the night, they took frequent junk-food breaks. The Apple crew would make forays to the all-night 7–11 store. When Woz got tired of walking around a long wooden fence, he pulled out a plank so they could just slip through. It was typical of his impatience. But it also characterized the way the company had to cut corners in the beginning and get the product "out the door" in a hurry, as is said in computer-industry parlance.

As a result, there were a lot of problems. The first computer cases had covers that warped, and the cases often had bubbles that had to be hand-sanded and repainted. Wozniak didn't have a power supply that could easily fit into Jobs's idea of a wide, flat computer case. Jobs called up a friend at Atari, who eventually put him in touch with Rod Holt, a company engineer. When Holt saw the Apple II he was as impressed as Gordon French—which is to say, not very much. Jobs couldn't get it to work right, and the two Steves' idea of a power supply violated the Federal Communications Commission's regulations on radiation emissions. Rod Holt knew they were desperate for help, and in a fit of some whimsical madness, left a very secure but not particularly stimulating engineering position to work at Apple. Holt found out right away that although Woz was brilliant at digital electronic theory, he was somewhat weaker in analog theory (which dealt with the more boring, mundane, but absolutely necessary side of electronic products). The power supply problem was left completely to Holt to solve because nobody else was qualified to tackle it.

Holt was perturbed at Woz's strange work habits. Woz showed up when he felt like it and often forgot he had to finish a project. Woz's mind was traveling at light speed, though, and it was in so many places at once that he became increasingly absentminded. He'd often start something that Holt had to finish. Woz wasn't much interested in tending to minor details. So when someone wondered how the Apple II would be cooled without a fan, it was Holt who sliced slots in the casing.

Meanwhile, Markkula had asked Michael Scott to become the company president, the man who would be the manager and oversee production. Markkula had known Scott since they both worked at Fairchild. Scott was now in a middle-level management position at National Semiconductor and looking to move up. He welcomed the opportunity. When Scott, also known as "Scotty," came to Apple he found that, sure, Woz was flaky, but look at what he already had accomplished all by himself. It was sheer genius. Scotty figured people like Holt could put up with Wozniak's eccentric workday. First off, he was impressed with Woz's technical ability in both software and hardware. So few people can think in the vast cosmic void in between, and Woz was one of them. Secondly, Woz's programming dexterity was highly polished.

There are basically two kinds of programming languages, high-level and low-level. The higher the level, the easier the language is for humans to deal with. BASIC, for example, whose acronym stands for "Beginner's All-Purpose Symbolic Instruction Code," is a very high-level language. The lower-level languages, such as "hexadecimal" (which uses a series of numbers and letters) and "machine" (which deals with binary code, the zeros and ones that the computer understands), are far more difficult to use in programming. In order to make life easier for millions of computer programmers, there are "compiler" programs, which are a kind of translating device. Only purists ever program in low-level languages any more, because it is extremely painstaking and time-consuming. But a purist would have one practical advantage programming this way. He would end up with a faster-running program that used less core memory than if he used a high-level language. A purist programmer who stayed up nights worrying about the hardware would program in hexadecimal or machine language. Steve Wozniak was such a purist. "We didn't have a compiler," Mike Scott Says. "If you can carry all that in your head, you're pretty good." Wozniak recalls the reason they didn't have a compiler. It was much too expensive—the cost was around ten thousand dollars to develop the conversion program. Apple really couldn't afford it at the time.

It was February 1976. They began working in Steve Jobs's father's garage. Bill Fernandez, who had the distinction of becoming Apple's first employee, was hired as a "technician," but his job turned out to be more of a gopher. "They were all chiefs," he said. "I was the only Indian." Fernandez spent much of his time running around the Valley picking up electronic parts. Occasionally, he tested circuit boards and ran experiments. One of his first chores was modifying the jack on a Sony Trinitron TV set so it could be used as a computer monitor.

The first real year of Apple Computer began in January 1977. There were less than two dozen employees. (When Randy Wigginton graduated from high school, the entire staff of Apple attended the ceremonies.) "We had the technical success from day one," Woz recalls. "We always were sort of the class machine." Everyone's role was pretty clearly defined. Holt and Woz worked on hardware, Wigginton wrote software, Jobs and Markkula went about selling the machine's virtues to dealers, and Scotty supervised production. Scotty also did several mundane chores at night—using cassette machines to copy program tapes, pasting corrections into the company's manuals. The company was still small enough that when everyone was too busy working, nobody bothered answering the phone during business hours.

"The Apple II's [the main circuit boards] were totally hand-soldered on the floor," Wozniak says. "There was no workbench." The machine itself was finally assembled on a conventional production line. Apple favored hiring youth because there were so few adults who knew anything about what Wozniak was doing. The first reference manual for the Apple II was written by Chris Espinosa, a short, blond, pimply seventeen-year-old who was excited about computers.

The Apple II was officially introduced at a Homebrew Computer Club meeting, and Woz explained how it worked. Later, he wrote a full description of what went inside the computer, entitled "The Apple II," for *Byte* magazine, which was published in its May 1977 issue. The article began, "To me, a personal computer should be small, reliable, convenient to use, and inexpensive." It was Woz's philosophy, simply stated.

A month before the article appeared, Jim Warren organized the first West Coast Computer Faire in San Francisco. "All the torn T-shirt hobbyists were there," Warren says. Warren had also founded a newspaper named *Intelligent Machine Journal,* which he later sold and which is now *InfoWorld* magazine, the bible of the personal-computer user. Warren still publishes the *Silicon Gulch Gazette,* a gossip sheet used mostly to promote his business interests. He recently wrote a piece in that newspaper which included a story about how Woz and Jobs arrived at the Faire looking scraggly and hoping to rent a glossy booth to show off their new computer. As Warren reports, the two Steves asked the show decorator if they couldn't trade Apple stock for a nice, prefabricated exhibit. They had no money. The man allegedly refused, preferring instead hard cash. When Wozniak heard this story, he categorically refuted it. Apple had plenty of money to show off its new computer, he says. It was another case of the legend clouding the less spectacular real story.

Despite all the chaos, all the long hours and hard work of starting a company, Woz still found time to express his sense of humor. At another computer show, he and Randy Wigginton pulled one of their all-time sophisticated pranks. They planned an elaborate scheme for which they invented a nonexistent computer. The two spent a great deal of time writing a yellow, single-sheet flyer announcing the "Zaltair," an update of the Altair, made by MITS. They had several thousand copies printed. The flyer's only truthful statement said, "You will not find the Zaltair in any store." There was an elaborate rating chart which compared it with five other computers, including the Apple. The rating numbers stood for absolutely nothing. Still, Steve Jobs was fooled by it. He showed Woz and Wigginton the flyer, commenting rather innocently that the "Apple didn't come out too badly." The two could hardly contain their laughter. It was a brilliant prank in one other respect. Wozniak always knew that the perfect prank pointed the finger away from the real perpetrator. He and Randy introduced the flyer with the sentences, "Predictable refinement of computer equipment should suggest on-line reliability. The elite computer hobbyist needs one logical optionless guarantee, yet." The initial letters of the words in the sentences spelled out "Processor Technology." Readers who guessed it was a hoax thought someone from that company had played the joke. The flyer included an order coupon, and sure enough, the MITS company received a few in the mail after the show. After the Zaltair ruse, Randy Wigginton became Woz's right-hand prankster. Randy specialized in putting skunk smell on people's chairs, giving the Apple factory a distinctly unappealing odor.

As stories about the two brazen young entrepreneurs reached the popular press, a number of romantic misconceptions were perpetuated. It was commonly thought that Steve Jobs co-invented the computer. In reality, he had nothing to do with its electronic design. In fact, he wanted to be involved as little as possible with the technical end of the computer. One early employee remembers that when they were particularly in a crunch for time, Woz asked Jobs to help with the design of the cassette port (where the programs would eventually be loaded into the computer). Jobs shook his head and blurted out, "That's analog. I don't do analog." He reacted as if the task was beneath him, when more likely it was beyond his technical ability.

One hardware project that the company was high on was a telephone-interface circuit board. It would allow anyone to subscribe to a data-base network and access large computer banks. All an Apple user needed to do was plug in the board and hook up his phone to a modem. Since the project involved a substantial knowledge of telephones, Woz figured Captain Crunch himself—who else?—would be ideal. Apple, namely Woz, decided to hire John Draper. Draper, however, was not the kind of guy who fit into Apple, even though it was going to be the one successful computer company that wasn't traditionally "corporate." For one thing, his appearance was a bit intimidating. He has manic blue eyes and tends to get very excited when he's talking. And he has scraggly hair and a longish beard. What teeth remain in his mouth are discolored and used to bite nervously on his fingernails. He is also a militant nonsmoker, and he got very upset when Scotty and Markkula lit up cigarettes around him. Also, Steve Jobs was trying to upgrade the company's image. He didn't think Draper was exactly Apple material. Finally, they stuck Draper off in a corner near Wozniak's desk, Woz being the one guy they knew would tolerate him.

Draper was continually pushed to clean up his design and improve his product. "Woz would take my circuits and chop off a few integrated circuits here and there," Draper says. "He'd say, 'I'll do this with software.' Or, he'd say, 'You can get rid of this nand gate by doing it this way.' So all I had to do was write the software that way and it would work. Indeed, it worked. I wasn't going to argue with the circuit. It looked like it could do just about anything."

He was right. One of the things it could do was allow the Apple II to be used for making free long-distance phone calls. It was a feature Captain Crunch couldn't resist. The computer would turn into a blue box. Eventually, the company scrapped Draper's design. "One of the main reasons they didn't market it was the fact that it could be used illegally," Draper says with a devious smile. "But almost any DCA microcoupler can be used illegally. Any of those interface boards for modems could be used for the same thing." Apple also frowned on the fact that Crunch couldn't tear himself away from phone freaking. It was a disease, and computers were simply feeding it rather than curing it.

But the Apple staff did manage to put the phone board to good pranking use, something that Wozniak had no qualms about wasting time with. Draper had programmed an Apple II to make 150,000 phone calls to find fresh codes for toll-free 800 numbers. "It just goes to show how versatile the Apple II is," comments Mike Scott. Woz also figured out a design for an auto-redialer (now almost de rigueur, in modified form, on today's sophisticated telephones) that would cause somebody's phone to ring incessantly. The person would answer and nobody would be on the line. As soon as he hung up, the phone rang again. Draper laughs as he says, "Boy, all I could say to anybody is, 'Never be Steve Wozniak's enemy. You could be in for a very poor time.'"

Little by little, software was written for the Apple II. Some of it was outstanding. Woz helped make much of it possible with one game he wrote called Breakout. It was a simple game that opened the way for all sorts of programs. Breakout is played by using a paddle to hit a ball into a wall of bricks. Each time the player hits a brick, he scores a point, and the score increases as he breaks through the wall. Basically the same game was already available in video arcades. Woz knew he had to plot dots on the screen that would give graphic displays, and he needed a couple of beep sounds (one for the ball hitting the paddle and the bricks, the other for missing). He knew he could write the program in integer BASIC. It turned out to be a masterful stroke of luck (or brilliance, depending on your viewpoint). "When we started, I put a few commands into the BA-SIC for drawing lines, graphic commands," Woz says. "And the ones I put in first happened to write the game Breakout. And, of course, that led to similar ones." Almost all of Apple's high-resolution graphics stemmed from that one idea. Today, Wozniak is pleased with the fact that Apple was the first computer to offer the particularly complete package, in its day, of graphics, keyboard, and ROM programming.

When Bill Bishop, an Apple programmer, wrote a game called Lunar Lander, the entire staff took off to try and get the space vehicle to make a perfect landing. Nobody got any work done that day.

Though Regis McKenna couldn't get the Steves to change the company name, he did come up with a way to polish the company's image. In one week, he had the corporate logo designed. It was a six-color apple with a bite taken out of it. The bright colors would remind buyers of the computer's color and graphics capability. It turned out to be an excellent move. The computer would redefine the industry's idea of a machine being "user friendly." Apple Computer began an expensive and extensive advertising campaign. It thought nothing of spending a month's revenues on a glossy two-page ad in a national magazine. The company finished building its first computers in April and shipped them two months later. By the end of 1977, it paid off its first big bank note. Some seven thousand Apple II's were bought in its first year. The company was already turning a profit.

Chapter Ten

Insanity Is the Mother
of Invention

Though the Apple II computer was growing steadily more popular, there was still one feature the machine desperately needed. For the computer to be really easy to use, there had to be a fast, simple way to load programs. Currently, the preferred method was to store them on cassette tapes. In short, it was cumbersome, annoyingly slow. The user had to run the tape machine at precisely the right tone frequency for the Apple to understand it. It meant fiddling with dials, and getting a program up and running was often frustrating. Imagine a television set that took ten minutes to warm up, and another few minutes before the picture appeared. Nobody would tolerate that today. An easier method would be to use a disk-drive unit, which could read information that was electronically encoded on a piece of Mylar plastic. The problem was that there were no such devices for microcomputers. One would have to be invented. Mike Markkula called in all sorts of consultants and experts. They pointed out the obvious and grim reality that designing one for the Apple II would be almost as complicated as the architecture of the computer itself. They spoke in "man-years." Apple couldn't wait that long.

In a way, Steve Wozniak had boxed himself into a corner with his neat, smug little Apple II computer. Sure, he had anticipated the future with those eight add-on slots. Someday, he dreamed, somebody would use one to hook up a robot arm. And he had cleverly designed Breakout, which proved to be an impetus for all kinds of programming capability. Breakout inspired dozens of whiz-kid programmers to write games for the Apple II. And though experts extolled the computer as a "business tool," people wanted computers to play games.

Still, the computer was selling well, and Apple was doubling its shipping almost every month. Apple Computer grossed $775,000 in 1977.

Right now, though, the company desperately needed a disk drive, and most of the available designs were for minicomputer systems and were large and cumbersome. How would Woz design a circuit board that would fit in the Apple? A disk controller card, he suspected, needed lots of chips. The problem dashed in and out of his mind during the last months of 1977. He effectively avoided the disk drive until early December.

Markkula had scheduled an executive staff meeting to discuss future projects on the Apple agenda. Woz remembers there were about twenty items on a list on a blackboard. At the top of the list was the disk drive. When Woz returned from that meeting, he immediately geared up for a single-handed design assault on the disk controller card and the machine portion that goes with it. He compulsively began reading manuals. A disk drive contains the only moving parts in a small computer, the motor that rotates the disk. It was tricky. If you screwed it up, there would be all kinds of problems. In short, the computer wouldn't work. "I'd never seen a step motor before," Woz confesses. Anyone else probably would have been in deep trouble. Not Woz. His wizardry thrived on innocence. Not knowing what was impossible would see him through. His inimitable electronic brew, the Wozniak alchemy, once again began stirring in his mental cauldron.

There was a big consumer electronics show scheduled for mid-January 1978 in Las Vegas, and Apple wanted to have a working model ready to demonstrate. Woz's incentive was the glittering atmosphere of Sin City. He had never been to Las Vegas, and this was as good a time as any to make his first trip. Woz was an amateur gambler, the kind who seemed to be successful because of instinct. Vegas would provide ample distraction from the rigors of integrated circuitry.

Actually, Woz had designed a disk circuit in his earlier days, but he just hadn't followed through with it. "You see, I had read a Shugart [disk-drive maker] manual," Woz says. "I had never designed a disk drive before, so I just looked in the Shugart manual and said, 'How do I generate all the right signals?' And then I started wondering how all the disk controllers had fifty chips. Thirty to fifty chips. So, I figured they must do something I didn't do. I pulled out a schematic of the Shugart SA–400—thank God, they gave a schematic—and I studied it very carefully. I studied the entire manual, and I learned what it did. I discovered their hardware did less than mine, even though mine used fewer chips. Then I knew I had eveything I needed for a disk drive. I had to solve a few disk problems involving synchronization. But I dug into it and a week or two later before the CES [consumer electronics show] I had that solved with a real clever solution. If I had known how it was done, I never would have done it so well."

Wozniak's explanation of his accomplishment is so modest that it is hard to fathom. Yes, he had some prior idea of disk-drive theory, but his system was such a vast engineering leap forward that it mesmerized all of his peers. His disk controller card took only six chips, and the drive itself is so compact it is the size of a cigar box. Woz had all but reinvented the computer chip by making many of the circuits perform tasks they weren't normally designed for. They functioned as things like shift registers and sequential multipliers. When he describes his feat, it is in a rapid-fire explanation which only someone who is fluent in digital electronics can understand, let alone appreciate. He is full of phrases like "jumping over five chips" and "finding new tricks to use flip-flops for." Those who weren't impressed by the Apple II itself were certainly envious of Woz's disk system.

The other incredible thing was that he did it in only two weeks.

The project was late enough that Woz needed some help. The long, arduous process of creating the disk's routines, or software, was left to Randy Wigginton, a fact which, he thought at the time, bordered on the incredible. "He had no idea what he was doing," Wigginton says of Woz's manic two weeks. "And here I am working on a quote disk-operating system. I had no idea what a disk-operating system was. I mean, shit, I didn't realize how a disk worked until we were doing it. Talk about engineers in a cage." The two worked sixteen-hour days, stopping only for junk-food snacks. After 11:00 P.M., they would drive to MacDonald's for a thick shake and fries, "sort of a reward," Wigginton says.

Woz and Wigginton were still working on the disk routines until the final days before the consumer electronics show. Wigginton remembers getting on the plane with Wozniak, arriving in Las Vegas, and staying up late into the night to help set up the Apple booths. They went on a crash schedule, working for a few hours and then hitting the gambling casinos for a break. This went on all night. They finally got everything working at 7:30 A.M., a scant hour and a half before the show opened. Wigginton was overwhelmed, being only seventeen at the time, although he was playing craps and blackjack and working as an ad hoc computer engineer. They decided they had better back up their work—that is, copy the routines on another disk—and Wigginton managed to screw this up, destroying a bunch of data. He worked feverishly to restore it.

Today, Wigginton can barely believe that Apple got away with what they did at the time. "Here we were announcing the disk for shipment, and the prototype was only held together through a prayer," Wigginton says. "If it had broken, I mean, only Steve could have fixed the hardware. And only Steve or I could fix the software. There were only like three [disk drives] in existence. It was working, but it wasn't near the final design." The production version would be ready to roll off the assembly line in a little more than five months. Randy Wigginton shakes his head; this might be one of the shortest cycle times—from conception to retail store in seven months—of any consumer electronics product in history.

When Wozniak is reminded of this hectic period, he concurs with Wigginton's version of the facts, though somewhat less wonderingly. He gives the impression that Randy exaggerates the hysteria. The way Woz remembers it, the disk drive was fully operational by the show's opening. "Midway through the first day we had it up and running," he says, smiling.

By July 1978, Apple Computer was soaring. When dealers saw the disk system, their enthusiasm was roused even more. The machine would be by far the easiest computer to operate. Ordinary folks, those with absolutely no experience around one, could learn how to use it in a matter of weeks. No longer was the computer a domain exclusively reserved for the hobbyists. As computers became less threatening, and more useful, the average American began to embrace them. The phrase "computer-literate" began to work its way into the media and popular culture. It meant that you did not need to know a bit from a byte to operate one. We began to hear phrases like "home computer" and "personal computer." Programmers began specializing in the Apple, writing games, mostly, but also other useful software.

Other companies began competing, too, making good computers. The CP/M (for "control program for microcomputers") expansion card was also developed. This gave the Apple's main microprocessor the ability to be adapted for use with thousands of other programs. It seemed like everyone wanted to do what Apple was doing.

A highly visible and respected Wall Street analyst, Ben Rosen, now an independent investor in high technology, touted Visicalc, a business program known as a "spread sheet." Visicalc allowed thousands of middle-level managers a quick, easy method of using a microcomputer to make financial forecasts. According to Rosen, the program would sell computers. And that meant lots of Apples. Steve Jobs still thought of Apple as the "people's" computer company, but he certainly didn't complain when Woz's machine was embraced by corporate America.

In Silicon Valley, Apple Computer became the darling of lunchtime electronic gossip. Who were those two guys anyway? Why, the two Steves had launched not only a computer company, not only a business, but an entire industry. In addition, they did it in one of the nation's most competitive arenas. Electronic start-up firms in the valley often went under before the paint on their signs was dry. Those original hobbyist computers, the Sol and the Altair, were gone, collector's items. Apple had crushed them. Sure, other new companies were jumping into the fray, but Apple had carved out the original spot. They were first and, as Woz pointed out, had the class machine. If you owned one of the original Apples, incidentally, the company offered to take it back on a straight-up trade for a new Apple II. (Ironically, this gesture turned out to be a better business move for Apple than it was for an original buyer. The Apple I is considered a valuable antique, and today it can fetch between ten and fifteen thousand dollars.)

Steve Wozniak now epitomized the new breed of electronics maven. Without knowing it, he had become an inspiration for thousands of Silicon Valley kids. He was a nouveau-nerd.

One such kid whom he unknowingly had a profound effect on was Chuck Mauro, a valley nineteen-year-old whose background was akin to Woz's. Like Woz's, Mauro's dad was an engineer at Lockheed. He worked on the Stealth missile program, and until it was canceled by Congress, Mauro's father had four thousand employees working under him. He met with the Joint Chiefs of Staff and even President Carter. Mauro wanted to be an engineer, like his father. But like Woz, he wasn't much interested in the formal training aspects, like going to school, for example. When he was only seven, he built a radio from a Heathkit. He won first prize at a small science fair a few years later. "I was the first kid on my block to have a computer," he says proudly. When he got to Santa Clara College, he spent his last $250, literally all the money he had in the world, on a

Kim computer. The Kim had been designed by Chuck Peddle, one of the early Homebrew members. Mauro, of course, had heard about Homebrew and regularly went to the meetings. He saw Wozniak demonstrate the Apple and went home enthralled. What a genius, he thought. It was the Silicon Valley style of hero worship. He bought an original Apple and learned how to program the 6502 microprocessor. When he read Wozniak's articles in *Byte* magazine, he was overjoyed. He had seen the author in the flesh, actually lecturing at Homebrew meetings.

Mauro was the quintessential computer junkie in college. In his freshman year he went through his clean-cut-student phase. Though he was an honor student, he was not comfortable with the formal academic atmosphere. In his sophomore year he went through his hippie stage. He wore sandals and smoked grass and didn't go to class much. He slept till noon and played with his computer. "I was a true hacker," he says. One of the first programs he wrote played the Elton John tune "Funeral for a Friend," from the *Goodbye Yellow Brick Road* album.

By the summer of 1978, Mauro worked up the nerve to call Wozniak. He wanted a job with Apple. He left message after message but Woz never returned his calls. One day, however, when Apple found itself desperate for software writers, Woz called Mauro back. "I told him I was a 6502 programmer," Mauro says. Woz asked him to come down for an interview. Mauro did, and he was a little taken aback. Here he was wearing a jacket and tie and everyone, including Woz, was dressed in jeans and T-shirts. Mauro was eventually hired for the summer. His badge number was fifty-seven, but there were only about forty employees at Apple. People had already left the company. His division, software, consisted of only half a dozen people. He immediately became friendly with Woz and Wigginton. He would have lunch with Woz regularly for the next eighteen months.

From day one, Chuck Mauro tried to set a precedent. He was a computer professional, albeit only nineteen, and therefore he wore a suit to work. Everyone wondered about this kid. He was taking his job so seriously. It wasn't long before he began loosening up, however.

Mauro certainly wasn't going to make the company's atmosphere more corporate. He and Wigginton brought a stereo set and hooked up headphones so they could listen to music while they programmed. Elton John, Emerson, Lake, and Palmer, and even classical Bach organ music got a lot of airplay at Apple. After six months, Mauro stopped wearing suits, and began playing pranks along with Wozniak and Wigginton. There had been a mice problem in the Apple facility, and Scotty went around setting mousetraps. Woz went around catching mice in paper bags. When he caught one, he and Chuck conspired to put it in Dick Houston's computer. Houston was a programmer, too, but an older fellow, and Woz liked to jog his sense of humor. It wasn't long before Houston's computer began squeaking. When Houston took the computer's cover off, "looking for a bug," the entire software division had a hearty laugh. When Houston became bored with the mice routine, Woz loaded one of Dick's cigarettes with an exploding cap. Woz took some mice home, and when one Apple employee asked why he was coughing and wheezing, he suspected his pets were to blame. But it wasn't enough to make Woz get rid of them. He loved the little rodents.

Scotty continued to push Woz into doing more programming and design work. One day, after prodding Steve for weeks to finish a small but long-overdue project for him, he began to get testy. Woz, although a company founder, was still an employee on the payroll. He actually worried that Scotty would fire him. No sense of humor, Woz thought. He's taking this much too seriously. He finally thought of a prank to deal with him. Scotty was the ultimate *Star Wars* fan; he loved to wear T-shirts with the characters' images. So, to buy some time and distract him, Woz called his office when he knew he wasn't in. He told Scotty's secretary that "George Lucas" was calling, and no, he wouldn't leave a number but would call again later. Naturally, Scotty was in a good mood, waiting for days for the film director to call back. Meanwhile, Woz finished his task.

Woz was happy with Mauro's work and gave him a raise at the end of the summer. Chuck went back to college, following the Randy Wigginton schedule of working at Apple mornings and evenings. But it just didn't work out. Either school or Apple would have to go. It wasn't an easy choice, but he dropped out of Santa Clara. "I just wanted to make my hobby my business," he remembers. And he felt a little guilty. He was the oldest of five children, and the only one who probably wouldn't get a college degree. Woz gave him additional responsibilities. He was asked to work on graphics. It was typical of Apple Computer's problem-solving. Get someone who doesn't look too busy to get working on the next priority product. "Here I was supposed to be a graphics expert at Apple," Mauro says, "and I didn't even know what 'hi-res' [for high resolution] meant. Nobody would do graphics. Not Wigginton, not Houston, not even Woz. Nobody would touch it."

Meanwhile, Steve Jobs's presence was always felt. He went around from department to department, checking everyone's progress, pushing employees to work harder. He had cleaned up his act physically—gone were the revolutionary beard, long hair, and sandals. Now, he wore suits and took showers. But he still had a caustic, adversary personality. "There was nobody at Apple that Jobs didn't call an asshole," Mauro says.

After he designed the disk-operating system, Wozniak was creatively exhausted. He busied himself on small projects, but none matched the intensity and pressure of what he previously had done. He was somewhat bored. The company's sales for 1978 were $7.8 million. The following year, Apple would throw a party celebrating its first million-dollar month. The 1979 gross receipts would top $47 million.

Wozniak and Jobs and Markkula and Scotty were quite rich. Only Woz was restless and somewhat unhappy. Everyone else was ecstatic with Apple's success, but the game wasn't over. There was perhaps only one thing worse than failing, ego-wise, and that was succeeding big and then failing. There was nothing more embarrassing than the prospect of being a "one-product company." For Apple to remain in the electronic vanguard, it had to look to the future.

And that's where Steve Jobs's specialty was. Though the Apple II was easy to use, it wasn't easy enough.

Computer literacy now took only weeks to acquire, but too many people couldn't spare those weeks. Jobs knew that to break down the last remnants of computerphobia, Apple needed to develop technology that would allow people to buy a computer, plug it in, and instantly become literate. Jobs took a team of engineers to the Xerox Palo Alto Research Center in December 1979. There they saw a demonstration of what Jobs thought was the key to his company's future. Xerox scientists had developed a method of using a computer that didn't require a typewriter keyboard to input commands. Instead, they used a device called a "mouse." The mouse, a pad with a rolling ball, allowed the user to move the cursor around the monitor screen and use software in conjunction with "icons," or pictures that represented different functions (filing cabinet, word processing, and others). The mouse, Jobs speculated, was what would distinguish future Apple products from the competition.

Jobs promptly assembled a design team to develop a new computer, code-named "Lisa." A forty-man team began meeting at the Good Earth restaurant behind the company's headquarters. It would take years to develop this new microcomputer, but Jobs felt the Apple II might carry the company until it was ready.

Woz didn't have the same sense of entrepreneurship. He wasn't that interested in building a bigger and better company. A better mousetrap, yes. He was an engineer at heart and not a businessman. Besides, he was pretty well burned out from the marathon sessions developing the Apple II. He was ready for a rest. His lot in life was not accumulating more wealth but fussing around with circuit boards. The money was fine, of course. He and Alice moved to a big house. He bought his wife a Mercedes. He treated himself to a Porsche 924 with a vanity license plate, "APPLE II." But he had problems getting the car's turbo system to work properly. His marriage wasn't working right either. Woz and Alice had less and less in common, even though he tried to interest her in some of his work. He bought Alice a small gift shop in Los Gatos to interest her in business. He bought a B-movie theater so he could take his friends to screenings of old sci-fi movies.

Apple began worrying about design secrecy, to Woz's

dismay. Steve Jobs became incredibly angry whenever the company's plans leaked out. One day Woz found himself at an executive staff meeting; Jobs was in a huff about some monitor code being all over town. After all, it was a copyrighted piece of software. Jobs slammed his fist on the table, and Woz thought that Jobs and Markkula were blaming him. Woz didn't know anything about the leak, so he slammed his fist, too. He never understood why they suspected him as the source of the leak. Markkula suggested that when they caught the guy he should be fired. Woz couldn't understand it. Much later, Woz found out that it was a high school kid who was working as a technician. "It couldn't have done a damn thing to hurt Apple," he says.

Woz's hours became more irregular than ever. After all, Apple Computer was now turning into the kind of place he disdained, a corporate bureaucracy. It certainly was a thriving one, but it wasn't exactly conducive to individual creativity. Wozniak found he would no longer be working in the hermetically sealed vacuum he felt most comfortable in. Now he was looking at a monster he had helped create, with this department and that, and design teams and projects.

It was a difficult time for him. He was forced to admit the garage days were over. The days of handing out schematic diagrams at Homebrew meetings were irretrievable. In fact, secrecy was more important than ever. Instead of rushing to a friend's house with a sketch of a new electronic design, you sent a copy to the company lawyer, who filed an application at the patent office.

Chapter Eleven

Apple Flies

Steve Wozniak thought about his money the way he thought about most things in life. That is, he didn't think about it all that much. He gave away large chunks of his personal stock to his close relatives and friends. His father and mother, brother Mark, and sister Leslie all received stock in their own names. Leslie put some of her gift into the Vanguard Foundation, a liberal philanthropic fund which attracted the offspring of the rich and famous. She sits on its board. Mark eventually donned a business suit and used some of his money to open a computer store in Sunnyvale. Margaret Wozniak has a new Mercedes which Woz bought, but she and her husband still live modestly in the Edmonton home. They would like to buy a bigger place, and Jerry Wozniak is looking toward the quiet days of retirement. Woz's unflagging generosity, his sense of sharing, is unsurprising. "Anyone who knows me knows that I can't say no, especially to my friends," Woz says. Many Apple employees were well taken care of, and the common estimates of the number of millionaires the company generated range from forty to more than seventy. Wozniak wanted some of the people who were peripherally involved but not members of Apple to share some of the rewards, too. He asked Steve Jobs, shouldn't Allen Baum get something for helping with the Apple II slot design? Jobs said no. Woz signed over some of his personal stock to Baum. In all, Wozniak gave stock to around ten people whom he felt helped the company attain success.

By early 1980, Woz's marriage was finished. Alice and he had nearly gotten divorced before, but now she had left him for good. According to their settlement, she got most of the material goods, the house and the Mercedes, and a huge piece of Woz's interest in Apple. She later turned her extensive fortune into real estate. Alice owns a 150-unit condominium and a property-management firm. She even has a large satellite dish antenna on her property. While her former husband's money left her rich, she became even wealthier on her own. Woz's friends refer to her somewhat disparagingly as the "Condo Queen," but Woz has no lingering animosity. They still occasionally have lunch together.

Steve Jobs's domineering ego was expanding like Apple Computer. His energy was infectious but his methods were overzealous. He gained a reputation for verbally abusing employees. Many around him were appalled at his behavior, yet some observers felt Jobs meant well. It was his method of extracting their best work. Coddling an employee might make him relax, and that was bad for business. Laziness, after all, could be contagious. Vociferously berating a worker would promote competition and the kind of tension that would turn out a good product. Others understood, if they did not appreciate, his bulldozing mentality.

Still, employees were afraid of Jobs. They thought he was a megalomaniac. The thought his impatience was rude and childish. He was the kind of person who couldn't believe he had to wait on line at the bank. Jobs felt everyone who worked for Apple should share his obsession. A while later he would run into a California legislator, Pete Stark, on an airplane, and after discussing business for an hour, he rushed back to Apple with a marvelous idea. Why not donate a computer to every public school in the U.S. with the goal of national computer literacy? Every kid should have the opportunity to learn about computers, and Apple should be in the forefront of this drive. Naturally, Steve Jobs had an ulterior motive. Apple couldn't afford such a grand gesture unless a new law was passed increasing the corporate limit for educational tax deductions. The "Apple Bill" proposal garnered quite a bit of publicity. It was typical of Jobs's macro-thinking. Jobs figured that computer product identification would become like that of cars. If a school kid learned computers on an Apple, that was what he'd eventually buy.

Meanwhile, other companies started to duplicate Apple's success. Atari and Radio Shack announced home computers, and IBM had long been rumored to be developing its own "personal" computer. Apple knew its model II computer might not be able to compete with the IBM. Apple still had a youth image that didn't wash on Wall Street. Lots of people would prefer the IBM simply because it was an IBM. The Lisa project was promising but not at all immediate. The useful life of a computer might be only a few years. The company had to think ahead, and the short term seemed to beg for still a newer version of the Apple II. It would be more business-oriented (to compete with the IBM), have a larger memory capacity, and also be more expensive. It would be called the Apple III. Wozniak, however, had little to do with it. The new computer was being developed by a design team, and that was hardly the way Woz worked best.

The marketplace was about to get crowded, and naturally, some Apple pioneers looked elsewhere for new opportunities. When Jobs heard about an employee leaving, he became positively livid. How could he? Where was his loyalty? Look what Apple had done for him. Jobs was obviously displaying his one-dimensional view of the world. Apple Computer Inc. was first and everything else was second. Why, Jobs had big plans for his minions—not the least of which was a huge tract of land called "Apple Park," which would contain not only the company's industrial facilities but also supply recreational, health, and housing needs. Sort of a Japanese "family" management arrangement.

Steve Wozniak realized that his own success had been brought about by working on a project on his own. So he, and supposedly Steve Jobs, gave their engineers the same encouragement. Come up with a product, and if Apple won't produce it, then you're free to set out on your own. Apple Computer endorsed entrepreneurship. After all, the company had been created in that spirit.

Chuck Mauro had always admired Wozniak's work style (if not his habits). Put your feet up on the desk, so to speak, and dream. Then get the dream into a schematic and build a prototype. Woz fostered dreaming. Try something out, even if it appears to be unattainable. Not only were many independent programmers writing Apple software, but engineers were also working on products that would be "compatible" with the computer—modems, monitors, printers, even other disk drives. Mauro was working in his spare time on an add-on board for the Apple which would give the screen eighty-column capability, rather than the standard forty-column format. This would greatly increase the capacity for data display on a monitor. He designed the board with Woz's philosophy in mind: wherever you can, eliminate an integrated circuit. Keep it simple. When he was finished, he showed it to Woz, who liked it. It would be a great product for Apple.

Mauro sensed it might be a big seller. He approached Steve Jobs to make a deal. Jobs said, "I'll give you twenty thousand for it."

"No," Mauro said. He preferred a piece of the action. "I want a 20 percent royalty on sales."

"No way," Jobs said.

"How about a hundred thousand advance plus 5 percent?" Mauro inquired.

Jobs shook his head. The two were negotiating like gentleman but had reached an impasse. Actually, they weren't even close to an agreement. Mauro remembers that he and Jobs agreed to discuss it again later. But Jobs suddenly became inaccessible, stalling him for close to two and a half months. Every time he stopped by Jobs's office, his secretary told him Jobs was "too busy." Mauro became increasingly angry. He wondered about Jobs. This was the same guy who used to work in jeans and walked around his carpeted office in bare feet. Too

116

busy? This was the same guy who two years ago would stop me in the corridor, straighten my lapel, and tell me how pleased he was with my work.

Mauro finally realized that "he was using time to try to break me down, to frustrate me." He nearly gave in. But he had a good product, and he didn't want to see it die on the shelf. He went to see Mike Markkula and complained that Jobs was stalling him. He told him that he'd consulted a lawyer about the eighty-column card. He knew that going around Jobs would eventually prompt some action.

"That got Apple's attention," Mauro says, "when you told them you had a lawyer." Markkula scheduled a lunch date with Mauro and his attorney, but then abruptly canceled, using a flimsy excuse. That worried Mauro; Markkula was not usually like that.

Finally, Jobs agreed to go to lunch with Chuck Mauro and his lawyer. It is one of Mauro's more vivid memories as an Apple employee. They walked across the street to the Good Earth, the health-food restaurant where the Lisa team met. Mauro and his attorney hadn't said a word when Jobs blurted, "You know, I could sue your ass. I could squash you like a bug." It was as if Mauro had double-crossed Apple. Mauro calmly reminded Jobs that a guy named Steve Wozniak had done the same thing at Hewlett-Packard not too many years ago. Certainly, the design work on projects not assigned by the company fell into that hazy, gray area. It belonged neither to the company nor the engineer, but to both parties. Lunch became a battle of loud voices, certainly unbefitting the spirit of the Good Earth. But this was business. Jobs told Mauro he wanted his immediate resignation. He went into hysterics. He threw all kinds of red herrings at Mauro, even to the point of blaming him for the fact that the Apple III was late. (In fact, it would be another year before that computer was unveiled.) Surprisingly, when everyone calmed down, Jobs agreed to give Mauro a release. The product was his, and he was free to start his own company. The irony of it all was that Mauro had to pick up the lunch check.

Wozniak was not interested in the internecine battles of the company he had co-founded four years earlier. He consciously avoided executive spats. In fact, he was not interested in much of anything except learning how to fly a plane. It was almost summer, his divorce from Alice had become final, and Woz was spending little time at work. He was doing some small projects with Markkula and Randy Wigginton, but they realized that Woz wasn't in his obsessive work mode. When they needed to reach him, they knew he could be found at the local airport, tooling around in a Piper.

There was one project that did kindle a spark in the old Woz. Steve Jobs had decided that there should be a companion computer to Lisa, a cheaper version with similar technology. In January 1980, he rounded up some of the company's old-timers—actually young engineers—and took control of Macintosh. Mac, as it was nicknamed, might regenerate the long-dissipated Apple energy. Woz began thinking about Mac.

One fortunate day when Woz did show up at Apple, he met the woman who was to become his second wife.

Candi Clark, twenty-six, had been at Apple for about a year. She hardly planned to work for a computer company, however. Her first love had been sports. Trim and athletic with long, light brown hair, Candi had spent most of her early twenties as a competitive kayaker. The daughter of a fairly wealthy building contractor, she never had to worry about needing money to train. She reached world-class status, earning a berth on the U.S. Olympic team that went to Montreal in 1976. She didn't win a medal, and although she hadn't yet reached kayaking retirement age, she knew she couldn't paddle around forever. She began to wonder about a career. She finished college and earned a degree in accounting. Her brother had been working at Apple, testing new products. He called her. Would she mind coming in to see if an accounting program was any good? She didn't. It wasn't long before she became a full-time employee. She liked her work and the company, too.

Candi, of course, knew who Woz was—everyone at Apple did. One of Woz's favorite evening activities was to invite staffers to his B-movie theater. In August, he finally mustered the nerve to sort of ask Candi along to a sci-fi screening. By "sort of," Woz meant, "Why don't you meet me at the theater?" She did, and after the show they went out for coffee with one of Woz's friends. This kind of indecisive courting went on until September. Candi figured that Woz had forgotten how to date, being newly single. Actually, it was simply Woz's shyness around women. Then Apple threw a beer blast—squirt gun party for its summer interns. Woz was busy making bootleg copies of *The Empire Strikes Back* on a videocassette recorder, and at the same time squirting Candi.

Woz said, "Why don't we go to a movie some time?"

"How about tonight?" Candi asked, figuring she might never get Woz to ask her out.

They passed on the movie and ended up instead at the Malibu Grand Prix racecourse in Redwood City, driving around in miniature racing cars. They had dinner and went dancing.

Candi left for vacation the next day, but when she returned, there were a dozen roses on her porch.

Woz was in love again, and this time it wasn't with a computer. They began dating steadily. She would accompany Woz to a computer user's group meeting. He'd spend a weekend watching Candi on a lake in her kayak. They rented a plane and flew to San Francisco to see a Paul Simon concert. At Thanksgiving, Woz and Candi flew out to Wichita, Kansas, to pick up his new airplane, a Beechcraft Bonanza, a single-engine, six-place aircraft completely outfitted with the latest electronic gear, including radar. The price tag was around $250,000.

December turned out to be one of the better months of 1980 for Steve Wozniak. On the twelfth, Apple Computer Inc. went public after months of anxious speculation by stock analysts. "AppleC" on the over-the-counter market was one of the hottest issues ever to hit Wall Street. The entire offering was oversubscribed at around $14 a share. In a month Apple stock ahd doubled. The shares that Woz had given to his parents, brother, and sister were worth a few million dollars; his ex-wife Alice Robertson had around $20 million; and Woz himself was worth around $50 million. (He has around 3.7 million shares.) The two largest individual shareholders were Mike Markkula and Steve Jobs with 7.1 million shares each. When Apple was issued, their net worth was around $100 million apiece.

Staggering figures for anyone, to be sure, but money wasn't on Woz's mind as much as Candi Clark. Apple traditionally shut down for vacation between Christmas and New Year's, and Woz and Candi decided to take a month's trip around the world, "sort of a honeymoon," according to Candi. By the time they arrived in Bali, they were engaged. But they couldn't tell their parents because they had trouble calling out of the country's primitive telephone system. That would have to wait until they reached Singapore, a more prosperous and modern country. Candi was delighted. When they reached Hong Kong, Apple dealers showed their hospitality. Woz was pleased that his computer was a success not just in America but in foreign countries, too. In fact, they found stores selling Apple computers everywhere but Bali. When a foreign programmer had a problem, Woz was eager to help him out. Sri Lanka was a special stop for Woz. He had always admired Arthur C. Clarke, the celebrated author of *2001: A Space Odyssey*. So on their arrival, Woz just looked up his phone number in the directory and they were immediately invited over. Clarke gave them his car and driver; they had a week-long tour. Woz even promised to send Clarke an Apple II—it had become his favorite gift—but, as was often the case, he forgot to send it. "Steve means well," says Candi, "but he overextends himself. He says yes to everyone about everything."

When the couple returned from their global tour, their friends hosted an engagement party. Woz and Candi had been living together in Scott's Valley, but they moved to a new house in Los Gatos, high in the Santa Cruz Mountains above the coastal fog. When you drive up to the gate there is a sign that reads "Candi and Woz," and after climbing the long circular driveway you come to another, "Welcome to the Castle." It is a turreted affair on a knoll, and off to one side is a lighted tennis court, a stable full of llamas, and a garage cluttered with motorcycles and dune buggies. There is a guest house where some of the servants live. There are four cars. Woz has a new dark-blue Porsche 928 and a Datsun 280–ZX; Candi drives a Mercedes 350–SL and a Volvo station wagon with her kayak on the roof. A pack of a half-dozen dogs yelps about the property. The swimming pool is an indoor-outdoor type. The satellite dish antenna sits on the hill outside the kitchen window. There's a lake. Inside, the house is roomy and comfortable. But it isn't opulent. Candi says that Woz is sometimes embarrassed that he lives in a place as big as this. But the decor is what you might expect from a computer engineer. There is a hooked rug with the Apple logo in the hallway and a small painting of his plane on the wall. The living room has one of those plastic-coated redwood-tree coffee tables. There are beamed ceilings. The stereo loudspeakers sit in the corners along with a projection TV screen and a robot (Nolan Bushnell's "Topol"). One wall features a panoramic wide-angle photo of Woz onstage at the US Festival cradling his son. There are several cartons of unopened fan mail; even a letter addressed only to "Steve Wozniak, Santa Cruz Mountains, California" has arrived at the compound.

To the right of the entranceway, there is a small office where Woz has a workbench, several computers, assorted printers and adjunct paraphernalia, an electric guitar, and his four coveted patents framed on the wall. Also hanging there are the circuit boards of the Apple I and II computers. His current software library sits neatly on two shelves. The workbench is tidy and has a voltmeter, oscilloscope, soldering iron, and an open bag of half-eaten Cheezits. It looks lightly used. The drawers contain all kinds of electronic parts, circuit boards haphazardly stacked on top of one another. The office is cramped, and Wozniak is in the process of moving it to a second-floor extension now under construction. Much of Woz's software is stacked on a shelf in a closet across the hall. Wozniak is a computer salesman's delight; he is compulsive about buying two of everything, one for hard use and the other to remain in its pristine state with the plastic still sealed.

"He's the best Apple consumer there is," Candi says of her husband. "Probably because of his unlimited budget. Any Apple store he sees, he'll stop in and browse around and buy stuff. I think he buys mostly at his brother's store, but he goes to all the stores in the valley. Plus all the consumer electronics. We have to replace everything in the house every couple of months with the latest something-new-that-comes-out-that's-better."

Woz spends a lot of time upstairs, in the game room. There are several video games; Star Gate, Tempest, Pac-Man, Tutankhamen, and Defender. There are boxes on the floor, "uninterruptible power supplies," with cables leading to the machines. Candi says the power service in this part of the mountains is unreliable, and the boxes will conserve a potential high video score in the event of an untimely voltage drop. "He takes his Defender business pretty seriously, sometimes too seriously," Candi says. Woz is not a violent person; in fact, he's the opposite of macho. Yet he lets Defender possess him. He plays every day, and a particularly bad score will result in his kicking and pounding the machine. His current best score is 265,050 ("WOZ" is punched in where you type the initials). His is by no means a bad score, but the high on the game is 514,000, achieved by a kid who did it during a Wozniak party two years ago. Several Apple engineers can regularly "roll over" (get the score up to all zeroes, effectively "winning") a Defender. It has not yet bored Woz.

About a month after Woz and Candi returned from vacation, they threw a party and showed their friends slides of all the exotic places they had traveled to. They were up very late that night, but Woz and Candi were still looking forward to flying the Beechcraft to San Diego. Candi's uncle, a jeweler, lived there, and he had promised to design their wedding rings.

Chapter Twelve

The Plane Crash

Steve Wozniak taxied his Beechcraft to the end of the runway at Sky Park Airport in Scott's Valley. Candi sat in the right-hand seat, and in the back were her brother and his girl friend. Woz revved up the engine and checked his instruments. Everything seemed to be functioning normally. He eased the throttle forward and the plane began its takeoff roll. After barreling down the runway, Woz pulled back on the control yoke. But instead of slowly climbing, the plane skewed off its flight line and rolled up an embankment, barely missing a parked helicopter. It finally flipped over its front end and crashed to a halt. Woz, Candi, and her brother were unconscious, their faces and bodies bathed in blood. Her brother's girl friend, the only one who hadn't passed out, thought she was the lone survivor.

When Woz came to, he was in a hospital intensive-care unit. His injuries were multiple: concussion, partial skull fracture, double vision, and amnesia. He was out for the better part of a week, and when he awakened, he didn't even remember the accident. Candi was in intensive care, too, and her face needed extensive plastic surgery, three operations in all. She still has a hearing impairment in one ear. Margaret Wozniak took Polaroid photos of Candi and Woz during their ten days in the hospital. They show two truly grotesque, nearly disfigured faces. When they were finally discharged, they went to Candi's parents' house to recuperate.

Woz, however, was nowhere near normal. "If you talked to him, he didn't know that you just talked to him five minutes ago," Candi says. "He was in that sleep-walking state for about five or six weeks. He'd say really dippy things, the kind of things you'd say when you're asleep, nonsense phrases. My parents went on vacation, and that's when he woke up. That was kind of interesting. He woke up in the middle of the night and kind of rolled over and said, 'Oh wow. I had a really restless night. It's been a long weekend. But we'll go to work in the morning. I had this dream that we had a terrible crash.' I sort of went along with it. I said, 'Yeah, that was a dream.' It was sort of dark, and he couldn't see my face. And then he said something like, 'Did we really have a crash?' And I said, 'Of course, we had a crash.' And then I turned on the lights and showed him all the newspaper clippings, pictures of the crashed plane, hundreds of get-well cards. He got really excited. He had a few memories from that period, but they were bits and pieces of that time. He didn't remember a whole lot of it."

Candi's and Woz's faces have been restored to normal, and Candi can't resist the joke that the crash actually made her husband better-looking. His crooked teeth were replaced, and now he exhibits a toothpaste-ad-quality smile.

The near-tragic accident still haunts Woz, as a legal nuisance. Insurance did not cover the extensive medical bills. Candi's brother's girl friend caused a major estrangement between the Clark and Wozniak families. First, she asked for $10 million in compensation. Woz thought that was an unreasonably high amount, so he refused. Now she is suing Woz for $3 million in damages, even though he took care of all her medical bills after the accident. She had whiplash, so Woz bought a hot tub. He arranged for a full-time housekeeper and also hired a tutor. Candi has tried to put her injuries in perspective. "Her pain is real," she says. "But she wants it to be there. We think she's a head case. We did everything we could for her, but that wasn't enough."

After Woz and Candi recovered fully, they were married in June at Candi's parents' home in Lafayette. Some five hundred "close friends" of the couple attended. According to Gordon French, "Just from the champagne that was spilled, you and I could stay drunk for a year." Steve Jobs was the best man. Folksinger Emmylou Harris provided entertainment.

The plane crash was only part of a bad turn of luck in 1981. Things weren't going well at Apple Computer Inc. either. One problem was psychological. Though the company was only five years old, it had been founded by young guys who wanted to have fun. "They only planned on making a few nickels," was how Jerry Wozniak puts it. "They thought if they made ten thousand dollars that would be a lot." By the time it went public, it was rolling along selling Apple II's at the rate of 25,000 a month (there are estimates of about a million in use today). Today, the firm's Carrollton, Texas, plant turns out the Apple II (now the IIe for "enhanced") at the rate of 120 per hour.

Apple was accustomed to doing things in a hurry with its whiz-kid mentality. But those halcyon days were over. Another problem was directly related to a bad computer. The interim follow-up product, the Apple III, was rushed to the marketplace when it wasn't ready. The first 14,000 that came off the assembly line had to be recalled for retooling. Early reviews were less than complimentary. When dealers began returning them because they weren't working properly, *Computerworld,* the trade weekly, published a story with the very apt headline, "Apple III a Lemon."

The Apple III had failed largely because it didn't have a singular spirit, a guiding prodigy like Woz. So many Apple folks had their egos wrapped up in the machine that everyone eventually compromised just to get it finished with. The result was a stillborn computer that really should have succeeded if it had been handled better.

Apple's administration had grown to the kind of bureaucratic proportions that made it unmanageable.

Randy Wigginton complained to *California* magazine that there was too much sludge in the way of unproductive employees. Basically, it was a one-computer company—in the finished-product sense—and if you were an engineer and weren't doing something Apple II–related, you were expensive—and nonessential—overhead. Wigginton called the new breed of Apple designers "Clydesdale engineers." By that he meant they weren't in any hurry to get something done that would be profit-making.

Mike Scott, seeing all the waste, went on a rampage, firing employees en masse and drastically reducing the number of projects. It all happened on February 25, 1981, a day which, according to *California*, was dubbed "Black Wednesday" and "Night of the Long Knives." Apple appeared to be crashing like Woz's Beechcraft. Less than half a year later, Scotty himself was eased out of Apple. According to Wigginton, Scotty had been a company president who was excellent at bringing Apple to a certain point of growth, perhaps a thousand employees. Then it became the mutant animal, too much to handle. While he was out of town, he was relieved of many of his responsibilities. He was forced to take a lesser position. Insulted at what was obviously a demotion, Scotty bitterly resigned, less than half a year after Black Wednesday. He had too much pride to stay anywhere he wasn't considered important. After all, he was the kind of guy who wouldn't think twice about having an employee's car towed from a visitor's parking space—even if the car belonged to Steve Jobs. Under Mike Scott's leadership, however, Apple had became a progressive company. He had eliminated the term "secretary," if not the duties of one, preferring to call these assistants "area associates." It gave employees more dignity. He got rid of typewriters and replaced them with Apple computers. Also, he had instituted a program under which workers could borrow an Apple II and work on it at home. After taking courses and demonstrating a certain degree of proficiency, they were allowed to keep them. Of course, he figured that Apple would benefit in the long run from brighter, more efficient personnel.

It was almost a blessing that Woz was recovering

from the plane crash and had little knowledge of the messy details of Apple's reorganization. Woz didn't like politics of any kind, much less office politics. Steve Jobs could be the ultimate hatchet man, a messy chore. That relieved Wozniak. He didn't want to lose any friends because of business. Woz judiciously avoided any formal position of power at Apple so he could remain uninvolved with this sort of thing. Still, he had to quit working on the Macintosh computer; the design was thoroughly under way while he was recovering from the accident.

After the plane crash, Woz, hungry to do something fulfilling, decided to try to achieve a goal that had eluded him for a decade. He wanted to disprove Mr. McCollum's prophecy about his never receiving a college degree. After some discreet inquiries, Woz arranged through Berkeley's computer science—electrical engineering dean to go back to school under an assumed name. He did not want special treatment, favorable or unfavorable, because of his reputation. He moved into an apartment in Berkeley and registered under the name "Rocky Clark." (The pseudonym was a combination of the name of one of his dogs and Candi's surname.) It wasn't long, of course, before Woz was recognized, and word quickly leaked to the computer trade papers. Steve Wozniak back in school? What could Berkeley teach him about computers? his friends thought wondered. Was it another Wozniak prank?

Ironically, Woz found returning to college rougher going than he anticipated. First of all, he was no more adept at the registration process than a freshman wearing a three-day-old beanie. The administrative procedures confused him enough so that he was shut out of a few advanced computer courses. Also, the courses he did take surprised him in their degree of difficulty. Though he stayed up late studying, he did not always get A's. He does suspect that his handing in computer-printed homework assignments may have caused some resentment on the part of some of his professors. He did not especially enjoy economics, thinking that the teacher was out of touch with the times. He did enjoy psychology, however, and his interest was prompted by his weird amnesia after the crash. He is excited about the potential relationship of the brain and computers. "Nothing's known about how memory is stored in the brain," Woz says. "I'd love to know where and how. I've studied this and I'm fascinated by it." He points out that researchers are trying to see if memory has something to do with the crystalline structure of teeth. When you lose your infant memory, he speculates, it coincides with the loss of your baby teeth.

Though the press has reported that Woz received his degree, it just isn't so. Berkeley administrators say that he has not yet completed the formal requirements. Woz insists, "I earned it, I finished," but then he gives a long, complicated explanation about not getting transfer credits he legitimately earned at other schools. He probably needs to petition the faculty to actually get the parchment sent to his home. Upon hearing this his father smiles gently and shakes his head. Jerry Wozniak says, "If I know Steven, he'll never get it. He'll never fill out any forms."

Wozniak's dismal record in coping with formal bureaucratic structure is well known, but it is often misconstrued to mean that he also isn't a very smart businessman. This, of course, is not true. While it easily can be argued that anyone with his kind of wealth could not possibly go broke no matter how bad the investments, it is erroneous to assume that Woz just throws away money. One associate pointed out that his ear is close to the ground in Silicon Valley, and he's made money on the stock market speculating in other electronics firms. There is a strong chance that even without Apple, Wozniak would be financially self-made and extremely well off.

In addition to his Apple holdings, he has substantial positions in three different high-tech companies, all of which were carefully chosen to reflect his personal philosophy regarding computer technology. One is Intellidex, an industrial robotics firm run by his old Hewlett-Packard colleague, Stanley Mintz. Jerry Wozniak says that Mintz approached Woz during his amnesia period, and that his son invested a lot of money and cut a bad business deal. Woz's father says he had it renegotiated. Woz, however, simply shrugs and talks confidently about Mintz's ability, saying that he would give him a million dollars any time to do what he's doing.

A second Woz-supported company is Electronic Arts, a software publishing firm based in Palo Alto. Electronic Arts is headed by Trip Hawkins, an ex-Apple marketing specialist, and the company concentrates on games, with heavy promotion given to the authors. The disk packaging is very slick, and it is clear that Hawkins is headed toward selling computer programs in much the same way as record albums. (They even have liner notes on the jackets.) Bill Budge, the programmer who wrote Raster Blaster, an immensely popular computer game, works for Electronic Arts, as do many other talented people.

The third outfit was started by Chuck Mauro after his tedious and painful negotiations with Steve Jobs. Mauro's company is Advanced Logic Systems, specializing not only in eighty-column add-on boards but in several other computer-upgrading products for Apple computers. Mauro remembers how he sold his Apple stock to start the company—"we're the first real Apple spinoff success," he says—when he had only four thousand dollars to invest. He limped along for awhile, then called Woz up to invite him over to see his little operation. Woz hadn't seen Mauro in nearly two years and was busy organizing the US Festival, but said, "Let's have lunch," and apparently meant it. Woz figured they'd reminisce about Apple's "good old" days. Mauro's ulterior motive was business. He was screwing up the courage to ask Woz for a loan.

Woz arrived on time, much to Mauro's surprise. He was never this punctual, he thought. They went down the road and ate a good meal at the Rusty Scupper restaurant and caught up on each other's lives. Meanwhile, Mauro's mind was wandering toward worrying about meeting his payroll, looking for an appropriate opening. He stalled and stalled. Finally, back at the company, Woz rose to say goodbye. Impulsively, Mauro nervously asked Woz into his office.

"Woz," he said. "How, uh, would you like to get involved with this company?"

"Sure," Woz answered.

"Would you like to become an investor?" Mauro then asked.

Easily noting his friend's discomfort, Woz replied, without missing a beat, "Sure. How much do you need? A quarter of a million, a half a million?"

Wozniak was not only doing a favor, he was also investing in a company whose products he believed were good quality and had a chance to sell. Thrilled, Mauro asked Woz to be a member of his firm's board, a position Woz never really achieved at Apple. "I considered it a great compliment to be asked," Woz says. Mauro set aside office space just in case Woz dropped in and needed a place to fool around with circuit boards. A desk to put his feet up. A private spot to dream, so to speak.

Yes, Woz can't say no, especially to his friends.

Wozniak was surprised to see more than a little backlash forming at Apple Computer. Though he was no longer active with Apple, he cared deeply about the company. Hey, he thought, I'm its best customer! Some middle managers at Apple thought he was committing corporate treason because he was lending technical expertise, as well as venture capital, to companies that ultimately were competing with Apple (after all, it sells expansion boards, just like Advanced Logic). Woz dismissed the criticism as unrealistic paranoia, but he couldn't help worrying that some people at the company wouldn't want him back. They wouldn't think he'd be an asset, and some day, he thought, he'd like to go back to Apple as an engineer.

Chapter Thirteen

Woz Goes Rock and Roll Again

Steve Wozniak's friends and relatives wondered what was happening to him during late 1981 and early 1982. He had finally recovered fully from the plane crash, and now he was gushing to everyone about how he was going to throw this huge rock concert. What had gotten into Woz? Certainly, he had learned the computer business. Rock music was something he knew absolutely nothing about. Perhaps, his friends thought, Woz was worried that he could no longer do it. Suppose he was an engineering burnout? Maybe he had just one good computer in him and his career was finished? It was understandable. After all, what do you do for an encore after you invent a highly successful computer and help launch a multi-billion-dollar industry?

Anyway, everyone around him was bewildered by his commercial interest in rock and roll. During the year he spent on the US Festival preparations, Mike Scott speculated, "I think he's now floating around with the attitude, 'what do I do next?'" Randy Wigginton, probably Wozniak's closest friend and alter ego in the past five years, shook his head sadly. He partially blamed the huge amount of money Wozniak had. Investors wouldn't leave him alone. There was always another business deal or scheme. "In some ways, the money's made him unhappy," Wigginton said. "I don't think he has much time for himself. It would be great if everybody left him alone and he could return to the calmer days. Before, he always got back to his work. Now, I'd be really surprised if he ever designed anything again. The shame of it is that he really doesn't know much about anything but computers." His father lamented, "This Unuson, this us-ness, that's not Steve." Mark tried analyzing his brother's actions. "What's the real reason behind the concerts?" he asked rhetorically. "He wants attention and to be liked by zillions of people." Allen Baum thought it was the adolescent in Wozniak still struggling to express himself. "Steve Wozniak likes to indulge himself with toys," Baum said. "Now he can afford anything. The rock festival is really an indulgence."

Woz was extremely impressionable, especially when he met people connected with the rock concert. Whenever he was introduced to someone who piqued his enthusiasm, well, that person was just the greatest, the best for the job. Early on, those who had met Peter Ellis, his business partner in Unuson, warned him there could be problems. But Ellis seemed committed, and he had a seductive, attractive character. It was a personality that easily swayed Woz. None of Woz's friends were particularly taken by Ellis, however. Even Jerry Wozniak, who met Ellis only once, felt that he was not the right kind of guy for his son to be involved with in business. "Our impression of him is that he says a lot of words and never says anything," Jerry Wozniak says. His wife adds, "I was already prepared when I met him. I had heard he was a con-person. I was prepared not to like him, but when I first met him, he was charming." Woz's dad felt there was only one way left to get the point across to Steve. He wanted to make him a plaque for his desk that had just one word on it: "No." He wouldn't be telling Woz anything new. ("Anybody who knows me knows I can't say no, especially to my friends," Woz had said.) He already knew about this affliction; he didn't need his father to remind him.

Despite losing a spectacular amount of money on the first US Festival in 1982, Woz was determined to throw another the following year on Memorial Day weekend. He did not want to make the same mistakes he made during the first one. Unuson would take precautions against gate-crashing and ticket counterfeiting, which Woz suspected had cut into the first concert's receipts. He would get top acts. His friends, sensing a repeat performance of the previous September's financial fiasco, thought he was flakier than ever. After all, hadn't he proved he could lose millions of dollars? Why do it all over again? It was sheer financial masochism. Still, Woz was actually convinced he could break even or turn a profit.

Though Peter Ellis's crowd had not gotten along with Bill Graham, Woz still wanted Graham to book the rock acts. Candi Clark puts it this way. "The last person who talks to Steve is how things happen. Say Bill Graham talks to Steve, and so Steve is all excited and he says, 'We're gonna go with Bill Graham.' Then the next day Barry Fey [another rock promoter] calls, and he's all excited about Barry Fey. So whoever talks to Steve and gets Steve excited, that's what happens. It seems so obvious, the next day there's a whole turnaround." During the first festival, Woz, had complained that Bill Graham's organization earned more money than any individual rock act. Fey actually did get the contract for the second one.

At Unuson, in a rather spartan office (except for two Apple II computers on his desk), Wozniak displayed a contradictory character that was obvious to everyone around him. "Some days, I'm so excited because we're doing something great," Woz said, his enthusiasm controlled. "Some days, I'm depressed because it's such a hard business. The computer business is much easier than the rock business. Some days, all I want to do is design computers."

While Wozniak was often disillusioned with the endless details of putting on the second concert, he took a respite by occasionally showing up at a computer exposition. Looking at new products, hardware and software, still excited him. An expo was a great way to cool out, to recharge. Once he promised to lend his name

and support to Advanced Logic Systems at a Comdex
fair (computer trade show) in Las Vegas. Chuck Mauro
spent most of the three days running through both exhibits and gambling casinos with Woz, and Wozniak
spoke at a breakfast hosted by Mauro's company. But
Mauro says they had more fun gambling. At the tables,
they both could relax from the pressure of business
realities and real achievement. One evening, Wozniak
played two-dollar blackjack and consistently lost. Mauro
was amused by it. Here, he thought, this guy has millions of dollars and he's enjoying playing for such low
stakes. At around 2:00 A.M., they went to a restaurant
for banana splits (junk food, of course), and after Woz
teased the waitress, he suggested they hit the tables
again. This time Woz played twenty-five-dollar blackjack, and when he and Mauro were ahead about a thousand dollars each, they called it an evening. Chuck
Mauro was quite surprised that Wozniak had become
a real celebrity. At almost every casino they walked
into, someone recognized him or asked for an auto-
graph. The first US Festival had given him a higher
profile—he was now known to many more people than
those in the computer business—and his Datsun commercial running during televised football games hadn't
hurt either. After driving the Datsun 280–ZX Turbo at
the concert (the company had been a sponsor), Steve
was so impressed that he promptly bought one. Later,
he volunteered to do a commercial gratis. Nissan agreed,
but he was forced to accept the actors' union minimum
scale.

After relaxing at a computer fair, however, Woz would
go back to his Unuson office, working on the cumbersome but not unimportant details of the concert. The
people at Glen Helen Regional Park wanted more money
from Unuson; last season's lease had expired. Woz ar-
dently wanted Bruce Springsteen to perform, so he tried
to woo him again. He figured it wasn't just money that
would convince the Boss. Not only did he offer him a
million dollars (as he had done for the previous concert),
but he added a substantial donation to one of Springsteen's favorite causes, the Vietnam Veterans of America. Springsteen again said no; he just wasn't touring.

Still, Wozniak managed to attract thirty-three acts,

including a few blue-chip ones, for the concert. The headliners were David Bowie, Stevie Nicks, John Cougar, the Pretenders, the Clash, the Stray Cats, Men at Work, and Eddie Van Halen. Only hard-core devotees had ever heard of the lesser acts: the Divinyls, INXS, Wall of Voodoo, Oingo Boingo, A Flock of Seagulls, and the English Beat. Bowie and Van Halen were the top wage-earners for the weekend, knocking down $1.5 million and $1.0 million, respectively. The stage was even bigger than the prior year's, measuring some 435 feet across. Because of his increased expenses, Wozniak raised the ticket price from $17.50 per day to $20.00.

When the weekend rolled around, the weather was much like it had been the previous September, with temperatures reaching the mid-nineties, and the air dry and thick and hard on the lungs. California smog was as pervasive as ever. Wozniak, as before, was onstage to greet the performers. But the concert's topflight entertainment and again spectacular sound system were overshadowed by a number of incidents that hardly reflected Wozniak's naive, utopian spirit of "Unuson." By the end of Memorial Day evening, 1983, there had been 145 arrests, 120 major injuries, and two deaths. One man died of a drug overdose and another was beaten to death with a tire iron. The *Rolling Stone* headline read, "Violence Mars US Festival." The San Bernardino County sheriff called the concert "an absolute mess." *Newsday*, the Long Island, New York, daily, referred to it as "Smogstock Festival." It called to Steve Wozniak the "George Steinbrenner of rock and roll." Clearly, the spirit of the eighties rockfest was anything but togetherness. Kids in the eighties were still very much like kids in the sixties and seventies. They wanted to get loose on the weekend, get rowdy, get stoned, and listen to rock and roll.

At least the Wozniak family could say they had a weekend of togetherness. Candi and Jesse, Jerry and Margaret, Mark and Leslie all took advantage of the limousine treatment afforded the top echelon of the festival's organizers. They moved about the grounds in golf carts. Margaret Wozniak thought it was wonderful standing onstage when Eddie Van Halen performed, though it was clear her husband did not think much of heavy-metal music. Woz's mother reported that the backstage area was packed with groupies. Everyone was ogling Valerie Bertinelli, the young TV star who is married to Eddie Van Halen. Woz's sister Leslie went to the country portion of the festival, but she apparently didn't enjoy being among a Confederate-cum-redneck crowd. These were not the kind of folks whom she spent time with at the Vanguard Foundation.

When the receipts were tallied, Woz and Unuson took another large loss. Wozniak had expected 800,000 to show up. *Newsweek* reported that 735,000 people were at the site, but the true figure was closer to one-third of that number. Woz says that crowd estimates are largely myth and hype, perpetuated by the law-enforcement authorities and reporters (and Bill Graham). "I just learned a lot about crowd estimates that are not controlled, that are in an open space," Woz said. "This year, we built in so many controls on our ticket count that we know exactly how many were sold and how many people were there, within twenty or thirty people. We know how many tickets were printed, how many were sold, how many people went through the turnstiles." The first day there were 50,000. There were 140,000 on the biggest day. Woz believes that perhaps a fifth of the 600,000 reported to be at Watkins Glen in 1973 were actually there. Crowd overestimates, of course, are read by the agents of rock stars, and this contributes to the often outrageous fees they demand— and receive. Even with all of Woz's scientific planning, he couldn't make the concert a financial success. He had lost several million dollars again. The exact figure wasn't yet available because ancillary sales were still in the offing (video, cable television, and feature film rights, for example,) but that hardly mattered. Woz was too embarrassed to mention the real figures. He never discussed the specific losses with anyone but close friends and family. Wozniak was disappointed, but he was arrogant, too. Referring to his huge losses, he told Barry Fey, "If I do this for another fifty-five years, I'm in trouble."

But our budding computer whiz kid, as the press likes to call him, apparently hasn't yet had enough. He'd like to do a third US Festival. If 200,000 a day show up, he'll turn a profit, he insists. But so far, nothing near that number seems realistic. "I'm thinking very positively of trying to get together a viable plan to have a third concert," he says. "I'm not gonna finance it myself, and it won't be the scale that the US Festival was. There is some money left in the corporation [Unuson]." In an interview with the *San Jose Mercury News*, Woz said, "Next year I want to enhance the camping facilities. I don't think we have to go strong with the music ever again. I think we can be just a good concert, headlined by someone like Bruce Springsteen, and just have a few groups a day for a couple of days. We don't have to be the finest in the world any more." But there he goes again, fantasizing about booking Springsteen.

If there is a third concert—and most of the people close to Woz hope there won't be—it will happen without the Peter Ellis contingent. Woz has finally realized what everyone has been telling him about the man might have some substance. He explains somewhat ruefully what happened: "Early in the year, I started to realize that every time I heard something from Peter [Ellis], very seldom did it happen, did it come to be that way. Also, I was shocked at the lack of controls for the prior year, particularly regarding attendance procedures and ticketing. We hadn't even kept the ticket stubs to check on counterfeiting. I hired an accounting firm to do a personal audit for me. These parties were independent of Unuson. I was largely uncertain about the financial operation of Unuson." Indeed, he's not even sure how much stock he has in Unuson—around 60 percent seems close, he says.

Privately, Woz is fuming about Ellis's handling of Unuson. Randy Wigginton says, "He's really upset over the whole thing, like Peter Ellis drawing a salary of eighty thousand a year and he wasn't doing anything. Peter also voted himself a bonus of something like another eighty thousand. Secretaries on Peter's good side would get a bonus of fifteen thousand. I mean, a secretary? And like the secretaries who were not on Peter's good side, who were doing their job, they didn't get anything. It was all according to Ellis's friends, just unbelievable." Adds Candi, "They had a blank check, and they knew it. Everything got done and the production came off perfectly. But it could have been done just as well for a lot less money. The most fascinating thing was Peter Ellis authorizing a half-million-dollar bonus to all employees, which Steve didn't realize happened. There was no call for it. They were unwarranted bonuses, and Peter arranged to give them out and told people to cash them immediately. He was being sneaky about it. It's kind of a sticky situation." Also, the two wrongful-death suits filed against Unuson also will not go away very quickly.

Though Steve has fired Peter Ellis and has his lawyers' checking into whether he can recover the bonus monies, he is finally realizing that Unuson management was a bad dream. He is closing his eyes and hoping that it will go away. "He tries not to think about things that he doesn't want to think about," Candi says. The offices in San Jose are still open; he's still paying the rent. There are secretaries on the payroll. The accountants are continuing to pore over the books.

While Woz was playing concert promoter, Apple Computer, of course, rapidly gained momentum. The company moved forward on Lisa and Macintosh, both of which had become pet projects of Steve Jobs. Jobs had been taking a beating from the press, which had hinted that he was a less-than-ideal man to lead Apple into the future. He needed both Lisa and Macintosh to become big successes not just for the sake of the company, but for his personal reputation.

When Lisa was announced, in late 1982, it seemed destined for technological glory and commercial doom. The machine did everything it promised. Jobs was confident it would revolutionize the microcomputer market, even though it would cost the company $30 million, and according to Wozniak, take "two hundred man-years" of time in research and development. Lisa was introduced by Jobs himself to much press ballyhoo. The price tag: ten thousand dollars. Marveled one Wall Street analyst, "Simply put, Lisa ushers in the second generation of personal computers." But it didn't sell very well. It had revolutionary technology with its mouse moving the cursor around the screen, but was priced too high. Later, company executives dropped the price 40 percent, but it was already too late. Customers who didn't think the machine was worth ten thousand dollars also didn't think it was worth six thousand. Clearly, Apple was heading toward competing in the office-machine marketplace, and it didn't have the same skill selling there as did IBM.

Macintosh was introduced earlier this year. During the Super Bowl, Apple ran a half-million-dollar commercial that became mired in controversy. The ad looked like an avant-garde rock video and featured a woman hurling a hammer and chain into a face on a huge screen, supposedly symbolizing Orwell's Big Brother. The commercial was an obvious dig at IBM. Jobs looks at IBM as the establishment. Apple is more utopian.

The Mac computer does much of what Lisa does for only $2,495. It uses 32-bit technology with the Motorola 68000 microprocessor. The main programs and high-resolution monitor are quite spectacular. (The first reviews were nearly all raves.) Randy Wigginton, who spends a lot of time bad-mouthing the company that made him rich, has a different attitude about the new computer. He worked like a dog on the word-processing program, called "MacWrite," and gleams, "Mac is wonderful. Everybody is going to want one." It may revolutionize the market. Major colleges are ordering the machine for their curricula. If the new computer is successful, it may ensure the near future of Apple.

In the past few years, Steve Jobs has been a wunderkind, at least as far as Wall Street is concerned. He has appeared on the covers of *Fortune* and *Time* magazine dressed, as it's said, for success in a dark double-breasted blazer. When Queen Elizabeth made a celebrated trip to the U.S., Jobs, still only twenty-eight, was invited to lunch with her in San Francisco. He likes to count former California governor Jerry Brown one of his friends. And he's been seen with folk singer Joan Baez.

Meanwhile, Steve Wozniak, despite his earlier fears and trepidation, has been welcomed back to Apple Computer Inc., drawing a salary, though he hardly needs it, of course. Everyone around him is ecstatic. He is working in a high-tech, triangular black building on the corner of Stevens Creek Boulevard and the Lawrence Expressway on the edge of Santa Clara. A large

Apple logo outside the top floor is visible from the freeway. Staffers call the building "the Bermuda Triangle." Much of Apple's research and development takes place here, and visitors must be accompanied by an employee who has a plastic card that is inserted in an elevator panel (like a bank card) to allow access to his floor. As Woz escorts a visitor to his desk, he says, "At first I was thinking, 'God, everything is so tight with these cards.' But God, this is still much better than a key, and having a guard on every floor watching who's going in and at what hours." A typical Woz observation. At first, he wonders about secrecy and privacy. Then, after rethinking, he realizes how technology can be used benevolently and efficiently.

Woz was asked if he wanted to manage the personal computer systems division of the company. It was, more or less, a token gesture to an old friend and co-founder. Of course, it was a bad idea. Everyone knows that Steve is a lousy manager. After all, look what happened to Unuson. While Steve will argue that the "product was good" (the musicians played and a good time was had by all), you just can't get away with managing a division and not turning a profit by saying, "at least the product was good." Thankfully, Steve said no.

Wozniak won't be specific about his new projects, probably because he's often unsure about whether something he's working on will become a product, and partly because he's a little bit nervous about company secrecy. Though he claims company morale is fairly good, it is apparent that his mere presence has had a positive effect. Steve Jobs has declared a hiring freeze, he says, while he himself is anxious to sign on new engineers, fresh talent. He is especially interested in finally convincing Allen Baum to leave Hewlett-Packard. It might have to wait. "Each division in Apple may need sort of a house-cleaning," Woz says. The accessory products—printers, disk drives, software, add-on boards—seem to him in pretty good shape. But Woz realizes the future has to be viewed more clearly than when he and his partner were hand-soldering circuit boards in a garage. "Hey, almost all our revenues are from one product," he says, as if it's some divine revelation. "Pretty much it's the Apple II. Macintosh is still unknown, so it's risky in that sense. Lisa's still not making any money. It's selling well, but it was expensive to produce. And we're about to see the stiffest competition ever from IBM." Woz is being optimistic but maybe not very realistic. Last year, only twenty thousand Lisas were sold, though they expected to sell fifty thousand.

But at least Steve Wozniak has begun worrying about things he is passionately involved in. His friend, Lee Felsenstein, who designed the Osborne I computer, the first portable micro, once had a business card that read, "Research Fellow." Felsenstein didn't want a title with any encumbrances. Neither does Woz, but he also doesn't want a title that might be construed too arrogantly. His reads, "Principal Engineer." It is just arrogant enough.

Woz is back where he belongs.

Chapter Fourteen

A Whole Lot of Shaking Out Going On

When Apple released its annual report for 1982, the figures said everything. Its worldwide sales were $583 million, an increase of 74 percent over the previous year. Though the business plan that Mike Markkula had helped Woz and Jobs draw up was amazingly brash, it almost came true. So Apple didn't become a half-billion-dollar company in five years, cocky analysts said. It took six. They were off by a year. Wall Street insiders are labeling the Apple story the success paradigm of our time. It was the youngest company ever to make the Fortune 500 list of largest industrial companies. Mike Markkula and Steve Jobs made the Forbes 400 list of the richest people in America. Some 3,400 employees work in facilities all over the world, including Ireland and Singapore, assembling Apple products. Programmers have written more software for the Apple II series (including the "plus" and "e" versions) than for any other single home computer. There are some sixteen thousand applications programs available. Also, more than sixty companies have begun manufacturing Apple-compatible products.

The past performance has been excellent, but Apple's future is still somewhat rocky. Adam Osborne, the flamboyant entrepreneur behind the first portable computer, abruptly resigned last year, and his company filed for bankruptcy. It made the front page of the *New York Times,* and analysts predicted it would start a trend. Dozens of computer makers were trying to cash in on the microchip "revolution." There were just too many companies making too many products and not enough people to buy them. The industry's rapid growth was abruptly slowing. Computers were probably as mainstream as possible for the times.

The microcomputer business is definitely a grown-up game, and the challenge to remain a moving force in the industry will continue to drive Steve Jobs. Though IBM appeared to be entering the competition on the late side, its Personal Computer now is outselling the Apple, and it has pulled ahead of Apple in total sales. Wall Street analysts, however, haven't written Apple off. It still did a billion dollars in business in 1983. Apple stock was one of the most active over-the-counter issues last year, peaking at about sixty-two dollars a share in June 1983, but now down around twenty-five.

The question most often asked is, Will Macintosh save Apple Computer? Woz thinks it will. "It's a great machine," he says. "Everybody at Apple who was working on one wanted it for themselves. So it's going to be very successful." Notice the Wozniak key to creating a good product. Design it for yourself.

Jobs was smart enough to predict the stiffer competition. He knew he would need new blood, a guy at the top with good managerial skills as well as marketing instinct. He spent a good deal of his time commuting to New York City trying to find a new company president to give Apple its future direction. Though Mike Markkula is still with Apple, he has always expressed the feeling that someday he would like to move on. He doesn't want that active a role in day-to-day operations. After a thorough search, Jobs found his man—John Sculley, the forty-four-year-old former head of Pepsi-Cola. It seemed like a logical choice. Computers were being marketed like soda pop nowadays, anyway. Dick Cavett sold Apples on television; Bill Cosby touted Texas Instruments's home version. Atari used Alan Alda as its spokesman. Why, even Macy's sold computers. Sculley wasn't that interested at first. But Jobs wanted him, and he usually gets his man. One source says that Jobs turned on all his persuasive powers, even to the point where he had to ask, "John, do you want to sell soda your whole life? At least a computer means something." Jobs's use of social guilt—though in the corporate context—worked. Sculley said yes to an offer of a $1.8-million-a-year salary plus the usual high-level perquisites.

Steve Wozniak, Steve Jobs, and John Sculley had dinner together last summer to discuss the future of the company. (Their waiter recognized Wozniak but not Jobs.) Everyone agreed there were some obstacles to overcome, but that there was an aura of light just ahead. Wozniak was impressed with Sculley; he thinks he'll be a good addition to Apple. Woz was even happier to be invited to all the executive staff meetings he cared to attend. This way, he figures, he can avoid bureaucracy any time he wants, and yet slice yards of red tape almost at will. Woz continues to go to Apple user's group meetings whenever he's asked, his schedule permitting. Even when he was on leave from the company, he flew around from city to city at his own expense to attend. So now he figures he's the highest-level executive at Apple with an open ear to the complaints of the end user. It's comforting to him to know that when someone asks why doesn't Apple do such-and-such, and the request sounds sensible, he can walk into Sculley's office and get a hearing.

"You see, I never argued at Apple, I never fought with anyone," Woz says. "I just didn't believe in it, even when everyone was yelling at each other and quitting and firing everyone. I'm the only one at Apple who hasn't made any enemies." And now he is being rewarded for that kind of nonaggression. He is one of the few people at the company who is doing exactly what he wants and has but one layer of management—the top one—to contend with.

Wozniak has few regrets involving his career with

Apple Computer. Yet he has mixed feelings about the
rest of the industry he helped to develop. Some of them
stem directly from the Franklin Computer lawsuits filed
by Apple, which dragged on for several years until they
were recently decided. Franklin had basically copied
almost all of Apple's internal software and hardware
and built a cheaper version. It sold very well. Apple
lawyers claimed that it was a direct and blatant patent
and copyright infringement. Franklin countered by
saying that the copying was necessary to remain "compatible"—that industry catchword again—with Apple
peripheral products. Generally, they argued, the Apple
computer is public domain, like a car. Anyone can make
a tire a certain size so it can fit any make of automobile.

"At first I thought they were really compatible computers," Woz says, "I saw the first ads, I was so happy.
I called my wife. I wanted her to buy some. I definitely
felt flattered. I can't tell you, I was so glad. Somebody
else saw this market and that this type of product was
good. I thought they had gone out and designed their
own. Then I found out they were just copies. All the
engineering had been ripped off." Woz pauses, gets
mildly sarcastic, and continues. "So, I represent Franklin Computer. I am their chief engineer. They will totally acknowledge that. I've had discussions with their
company president and he acknowledges that I was the
chief engineer. I don't know why somebody didn't design a compatible Apple II. I could." At least they could
have changed a chip or something, he figured.

The case appeared to be a precedent in the industry,
and therefore it was bogged down in the civil courts
for some time. Finally, Apple won one suit. Franklin
was ordered to pay $2.5 million in damages, a figure
which probably covered Apple's legal expenses. More
importantly, Franklin had to cease and desist from
distributing software copyrighted by Apple.

Though Woz is happily ensconced once again at Apple, his ambitions do not always jibe with those of Steve
Jobs. Jobs is a classic empire-builder. He is demanding,
and he enjoys the spirit of business competition and
free enterprise. He is the kind of guy who rents Dis-
neyland for the evening for a computer show party. His
personal success and ambition are one thing. That he

wants Apple to remain a leading company is something else. He would like to take on IBM again, though he seems to have lost the first round. Apple recently purchased for $10 million a large tract of property in South San Jose, the Coyote Valley area. In the mid-eighties, it will become the company headquarters, though Apple still plans to keep its Singapore and Ireland plants. Jobs might yet realize his dream of "Apple Park." It might seem utopian, or even totalitarian, depending on one's view, but in either case it is a lofty goal.

Woz, in contrast, is not that competitive. Sure, he wants his company to continue to flourish. But he likes to be involved at the gut level of a machine. For example, there's no way you'll catch him putting three hundred chips into a computer, like IBM does. When he sees that many chips, he's convinced that at least one will burn out once a month. He gets "scared" when he sees too many chips. When he heard from a dealer that more IBM computers were returned for repair than Apples, he was very proud. He likes reliability. But he's not all that interested in going out and selling. And he's already fantasizing about pursuing personal projects, some of which do not have any chance of becoming viable commercial products. "I want to build a machine that will calculate e [a mathematical constant, like pi] to a billion digits with very low-cost components," he says. It makes his friends wonder if this is the beginning of a typical Wozniak prank. "There's no market for a machine like this," he continues in a serious tone. "It may end up being capable of doing other things, but there's no market for it." The printout alone would consume 220,000 pages. It would take three months to do the actual calculating—twice that time if he wanted to do pi. "Little bits and pieces of my whole life have gone in that direction. I've actually done a lot of the work already, calculations." Who cares if you do all that work and find out that the billionth digit is six or seven? Nobody, really, except Steve Wozniak. You see, it's not the score that counts, it's getting to play the game.

In a more practical area, Wozniak has been thinking in terms of software. He might someday invent his own computer language, "one that combines the best aspects of BASIC, PASCAL, and FORTH. There are things about each of them that are objectionable." And, he adds, it would be beneficial to keep the best parts of all three. By that, he means the "syntax" of PASCAL, the "globalness" of BASIC, and the "immediate testability" of FORTH.

Woz's idea would make programming more accessible to the average person. "It's just time to take the things we like about these major languages and combine them," he says. "The programming world is so formal and so pure that the word 'standard' is more crucial than in programming languages that are standardized, BASIC, PASCAL, and even FORTH. All these languages were standardized before today's personal computer–application software. They had no idea what software would exist." What Woz is saying, perhaps, is that we're living in a microcomputer world of Babel, and too many programmers are speaking in different tongues. So far, for the reasons he mentions, different languages are necessary. But it doesn't mean that this is how things have to be.

Along with Woz's dreams, he loves his role as a microcomputer emissary, and he plays it very well. In September 1983, Woz gladly accepted an invitation to speak at an IBM-Apple computer fair sponsored by the United Nations International School in New York City. He was dressed comfortably, in jeans and a navy blue shirt, a thin gold chain around his neck, the omnipresent Apple buckle latching his belt. When fairgoers introduced themselves and wanted to chat, he patiently obliged. He wore a polite smile. One man in a gray business suit was apparently overwhelmed. He said, with a slight trace of a foreign accent, "I saw you on "Nightline" on television. It's an honor to meet someone like you." Little ones asked for autographs and Woz happily signed his name. A local crew from a cable TV station interviewed him. An older gentleman carrying a "Save the Earth" flag appealed to Woz for support.

Before his speech, as is his wont, he toured the fair's exhibits. One booth particularly attracted his attention. A man was demonstrating an add-on circuit board for the Apple II series which allowed the computer to do a variety of things, including speech synthesis, voice recognition, and also to control several household appliances like a clock, stereo amplifier, and calendar. Woz's insight—designing the computer with expansion slots for functions not yet invented—was paying off. And nothing made him happier than to see other people go into business, even in one-man enterprises, because of his computer. The circuit board cost $495 and was named "Waldo."

To demonstrate Waldo, the man spoke into a microphone hooked into the computer and asked, "What time is it?"

The computer replied in an unmistakably robot-like tone, "Forty-six minutes after two o'clock." Woz smiled approvingly, his eyes beaming behind thick wire-rim glasses. "I think it's great," Woz said. "I'll buy two. Can I get two and take them with me?" The man, who was president of the company, nodded. He was, unlike his computer, speechless. Sure, he knew who it was.

A few minutes later, Woz gave his speech, in a small auditorium filled with about five hundred people. He spoke very quickly but confidently, and most of his comments were without benefit of notes. Mostly, he confined his talk to the history of Apple Computer. He explained that he only wanted to build a computer to play with at home, that his partner Steve Jobs was the salesman, and that neither of them knew very much about business. They "stumbled" onto a good thing. Suddenly, they had an "infant product." The industry was—and still is—very "unpredictable." "A lot of it was luck," he said, looking up from the lectern, as if he were waiting for someone in the audience to contradict him. It reminded me of a remark Woz's brother had made a year earlier. He had said, with an incredulous expression, "I don't know who was luckier, Jobs or my brother." Wozniak's mother had also quietly told me, "There would never have been an Apple if it had been just one Steve." She confided this at a time when Woz was not as well known as Steve Jobs. The Wozniak family admitted that they were slightly unhappy about the fact that Jobs was given credit for doing things on the Apple that he actually hadn't done.

Woz sprinkled his remarks with tales of the Homebrew Computer Club, and he described in some detail his numerous pranks. After fifty minutes, he received a warm round of applause and opened the discussion for questions from the audience. Most queries were fairly technical, a few about the future of Apple. One person asked why Apple stock seemed to move up and down so frenetically. It was a silly question, to be sure, and the man asked it as if Steve Wozniak had some powerful way to peer into the future. Perhaps Woz was thinking, well, the people who made Apple happen were frenetic, and they had their highs and lows, too, and they preferred to move quickly.

The man was fishing for a clue, for some valuable morsel of inside information: should we buy Apple stock right after IBM announces its new computer (meaning the PCjr)? Woz paused for a moment, taking the question more seriously than anyone in the auditorium. Finally, he just said he didn't know.

Epilogue

During the research for this book, I tried to interview one Berkeley professor of computer science who had had Steve Wozniak as a student when he returned as "Rocky Clark," ordinary student. The professor declined an interview on the grounds that he respected Woz's privacy—why else would he go to school under an assumed name?—and, anyway, he wasn't sure he could say anything about him that might help me. While talking on the phone, however, he did say that he thought Woz's invention was phenomenal, one that would have an impact for many years in the future on the way we view these machines. "I think we'll look back and see that Woz brought us the Model A Ford of computers," he said. His point was, naturally, that Wozniak created a product that might some day be viewed as indispensable and also could be afforded by common, middle-class people. Later, I mentioned this remark to Wozniak, and he said, sure, it was an interesting analogy. "But I like to think of the Apple II as the Volkswagen Beetle of computers," he said. In retrospect, both are pretty good comparisons. Woz, however, was thinking even more metaphorically. The VW Beetle was reliable, small, compact, and inexpensive. The Apple set a trend in the seventies for small-computer design, as the bug had done for small cars a decade earlier. And it's legacy will always be felt. You still see lots of Beetles on the road. In years to come, people will still be using Apple IIs.

Most of the people involved in this story are still active in several areas of the computer business.

Randy Wigginton, twenty-four, is an independent software consultant and multimillionaire. He employs several people to help him with his work, and he recently completed writing the word-processing program for Macintosh, Apple's newest computer. He hasn't yet received a college degree. "I'm on the twenty-seven-year plan, I guess," he says, a little more amused than embarrassed about it. He drives a Datsun sports car or Wozniak's old Porsche, and when he has time, sits in his backyard hot tub sipping wine.

Mark Wozniak sells IBM and Apple computers in his Sunnyvale store. For the period when Steve was away from Apple, Mark was his prime source of company gossip. His brother pays full retail prices.

Jerry Wozniak plans to become a computer consultant when he retires from Lockheed. He does not want to "retire to the TV set," but he would welcome the kind of freedom that would allow him to just pull off the highway and go to the beach on an impulse. When asked if he'd ever consider working on a computer project with his son, he smiles, and says probably not. Their personalities would clash. Margaret Wozniak says of her son, "Maybe he'll design a computer for his mother some day. She wants to learn how to use one, too."

Chuck Mauro, twenty-five, president of Advanced Logic Systems, says his company will do between $6 million and $8 million for fiscal 1983. Not Apple, but not too bad either. He likes wearing Yves Saint Laurent clothes because he likes the cut and they feel comfortable. He drives a new Cadillac with the license plate "ALS PRES." He is sincere and enthusiastic, and when he showed me a new CP/M card for the Apple, he proudly said, "This thing is faster than most PDP–11's [a very expensive minicomputer]." When he thinks about Apple, he likes to compare it to rock and roll. "Apple's success story is like the Beatles," he says. "There will be other rock groups, just like there will be other personal-computer companies. But it will never happen like that again." One of his key employees is Rick Auricchio, also an early Apple staffer. He flies a plane just like Wozniak's, and parks it at the same airport.

John Draper, forty, a.k.a. "Captain Crunch," is an independent software author who lives part-time in Hawaii. He would like to start a commune of software writers there. He wrote part of the Easy Writer word-processing program for IBM while serving time in jail for blue-box offenses. He spends most of his time in front of a computer screen and takes frequent walks on the beach. He drives a Mercedes-Benz.

Jim Warren, the originator of the West Coast Computer Faire and founder of *InfoWorld*, the small-computer industry's bible, has sold out his interests in both businesses. He is investigating ways to use the commercial airwaves to transmit computer signals. At the 1982 Faire in San Francisco, the last one he organized, he could be found wending his way through the crowd on roller skates, holding a walkie-talkie.

Mike Scott, the former president of Apple, is now in the space business. His firm, Starstruck, is working on launching a rocket which will eventually carry satellites. He is extremely wealthy, and when he's not at work, he spends much of his time on the phone with his broker. Woz was a recent investor in Starstruck.

Paul Terrell, the man who gave Apple its first order, now runs a software publishing company in Silicon Valley called Romox. The site of the first Byte Shop is now a pornographic bookstore, which, he says, laughing cynically, may say something about the future of the computer business.

Lee Felsenstein, the former emcee of Homebrew and principal architect of the first portable computer, is looking for work now that his Osborne stock has substantially diminished in value following the company's bankruptcy.

Jesse John Clark, the youngest Wozniak, is now two years old. He has been to two US Festivals, his favorite rock group is the Pretenders, and he took his first steps in Randy Wigginton's kitchen. Randy coaxed him across the room with a cookie. While this was happening, his father was playing Defender. His mother is retired from competitive kayaking, although she took her husband to the world championships in Italy. Woz, she says, was surprised and happy to see so many Apple dealers there.

Nobody is sure what happened to Ron Wayne, the original third partner of Apple who sold his interest for eight hundred dollars.

Steve Jobs, twenty-eight, the chairman of Apple Computer Inc., reportedly has political ambitions. Randy Wigginton thinks he would never settle for starting small, say a Congressional seat, but would prefer to win the California governorship. "Anyway, we're safe for five or six years," Wigginton says. "You have to be thirty-five to be president." Jobs rarely grants interviews (except for promoting the Macintosh during its introduction earlier this year), especially since *Time* magazine published a somewhat uncomplimentary piece about him entitled "The New Book of Jobs."

Steve Wozniak, now thirty-four, has settled into a routine workday. The way he puts it, "I have more than the normal amount of interruptions, meetings, interviews, so I'm pretty much only able to spend even less than half my day doing things I really want to do here. Pretty much that's opening up manuals, conceptualization, computer design, deciding what chips to use. After a few weeks of thinking about it, I put it down on paper on a very rough level. I do a lot of my work at home now. Generally, when you get to the breadboard stage with a soldering iron, then you're up till three in the morning. When you're looking for bugs, be it software or hardware, you're looking for sleep. There's been no change in me." Wozniak has never had a technician lay out his printed circuit boards, and says he never will. He has too much fun doing it. He's like a surgeon who refuses to let the junior physician finish the sutures. Woz has a secretary, but he frequently answers the phone himself. He types his own letters, on the rare occasions when he writes them.

Once I asked Woz whether he thought Apple Computer was now the kind of company where a young, upstart engineer like he was years ago at Hewlett-Packard would have trouble convincing his superiors he had a good idea for a product. "Yeah, we probably wouldn't notice it," he said. Then he went on to say he hoped that Apple would do for the engineer what H-P did for him; grant him a quick legal release and wish him good luck. He laughed and added, "The only thing I wouldn't want to do is finance it. I get a hundred requests a day."

When he was asked to donate money to renovate the Homestead High School baseball field, he happily wrote a check for two thousand dollars.

Since his plane crash, Woz has hardly been at the controls of his new Beechcraft for more than a couple of hours. His mother refuses to talk with him about his flying. When Wozniak thinks about his own death, he says he'd prefer to go in a motorcycle accident.

In 1979, Steve Wozniak was given the Grace Murray Hopper Award for outstanding achievement in computing for someone under thirty from the Association of Computing Machinery.

Much of the romance of designing computers is gone, Wozniak says. But his lyricism and wonderful optimism about these machines will always be with him. I heard him describe what he did to a layman this way: "There's a magic spirit of what a computer can do that you have in your head."

THE COMPUTER DATA AND DATABASE SOURCE BOOK

Matthew Lesko

A complete encyclopedia of *all* commercial and public sources of information for use with *any* computer. An indispensable tool for the eighties, this is *the* primary reference work for all computer makes and models, and all languages:

- OVER 1000 COMMERCIAL DATABASES—all current commercial databases are listed by subject and include names, addresses, phone numbers, and the fee for their use.

- *ALL* PUBLIC DATABASES—The U.S. government spends billions of dollars compiling data on a wide variety of subjects, from nutrition to stock prices, consumer trends to crime statistics. This information is available—and it's usually free. THE COMPUTER DATA AND DATABASE SOURCE BOOK explains where and how to get it, as well as listing the names and addresses of data experts who can help interpret the information.

- HUNDREDS OF DATA SERIES, including studies of such subjects as average professional salaries and tax rates for all major metropolitan areas.

Also included are tips on how to use the Freedom of Information Act, how to turn a government database into a commercial database for profit...and much, much more.

86942-X/$9.95

An AVON Paperback